"When we reach the diner, you'd better not stop."

"Are you crazy? I'm hungry," Silvio complained.

"We're being followed."

From the terror-filled glance the mobster gave him, Bolan guessed the older man had been away from action for a long time.

As the Oldsmobile neared the exit to the restaurant, the driver of the sedan realized that he'd been made. He gunned the engine to pull ahead of the Olds.

"Move it, Silvio!" Bolan shouted, drawing the Desert Eagle from its shoulder rigging.

Silvio spun the wheel and stepped on the accelerator, maneuvering the Olds just ahead of the pursuit vehicle with a squeal of tires. He roared onto the two-lane highway that skirted the diner, pedal to the floor.

But the sedan stuck to them like a shadow, and when the gap between the two cars had narrowed to a hundred yards, the gunner in the chase car opened fire. The Executioner returned fire, but couldn't score a hit on the weaving vehicle.

Silvio suddenly uttered a strangled cry and clutched at his chest, collapsing against the steering column. The Olds drifted to the left, straight into the oncoming traffic.

MACK BOLAN®

The Executioner

DON PENDLETON'S
THE EXECUTIONER

FEATURING MACK BOLAN

WHITE LINE WAR

A GOLD EAGLE BOOK FROM
WORLDWIDE.

TORONTO · NEW YORK · LONDON · PARIS
AMSTERDAM · STOCKHOLM · HAMBURG
ATHENS · MILAN · TOKYO · SYDNEY

First edition February 1990

ISBN 0-373-61134-X

Special thanks and acknowledgment to
Kirk Sanson for his contribution to this work.

Printed in U.S.A.

The road to hell is easy to travel.

—Bion,
from *Diogenes Laertius*

The highway to hell has no speed limit, and I'll make sure that anyone who chooses to travel that road makes it a one-way trip.

—Mack Bolan

THE
MACK BOLAN®
LEGEND

Nothing less than a war could have fashioned the destiny of the man called Mack Bolan. Bolan earned the Executioner title in the jungle hell of Vietnam.

But this soldier also wore another name—Sergeant Mercy. He was so tagged because of the compassion he showed to wounded comrades-in-arms and Vietnamese civilians.

Mack Bolan's second tour of duty ended prematurely when he was given emergency leave to return home and bury his family, victims of the Mob. Then he declared a one-man war against the Mafia.

He confronted the Families head-on from coast to coast, and soon a hope of victory began to appear. But Bolan had broken society's every rule. That same society started gunning for this elusive warrior—to no avail.

So Bolan was offered amnesty to work within the system against terrorism. This time, as an employee of Uncle Sam, Bolan became Colonel John Phoenix. With a command center at Stony Man Farm in Virginia, he and his new allies—Able Team and Phoenix Force—waged relentless war on a new adversary: the KGB.

But when his one true love, April Rose, died at the hands of the Soviet terror machine, Bolan severed all ties with Establishment authority.

Now, after a lengthy lone-wolf struggle and much soul-searching, the Executioner has agreed to enter an ''arm's-length'' alliance with his government once more, reserving the right to pursue personal missions in his Everlasting War.

Prologue

"Hey, Angelo. Are we stopping to eat, or what?"

"Keep your shirt on, Rinaldo. We'll stop when I say so. I know a spot that serves the best food on I-95."

"Yeah, sure. I always get heartburn when we make a run."

Angelo tuned out his companion's complaining and concentrated on his driving. He'd been making deliveries for his boss, Joey "The Fatman" Pinolla, for three years, and he hadn't kept the job by getting into accidents.

The courier pushed his Chevrolet along with the rest of the traffic, not calling any attention to himself by traveling either too fast or too slow. He scanned the mirrors, watching for the highway patrol. With more than five million dollars' worth of cocaine stashed in the trunk, Angelo wasn't anxious to have a nosy cop pull him over.

If he ran into trouble, then he and Rinaldo, the muscle-bound enforcer beside him, would try to bribe their way out of the situation with the large roll of cash he carried. If that failed, the cop was dead.

The Fatman wouldn't be happy about that. Pinolla controlled the movement of cocaine along the interstate from Miami to New York. The Mafia don distributed the powder at wholesale prices to his brethren, taking a small cut in return for the risk. The arrangement was both satisfactory and profitable for all concerned.

Success in the enterprise had been founded on good planning and avoiding trouble. Pinolla took pains to impress upon his drivers the necessity of keeping their distance from the police and of using violence only as a last resort.

Angelo glanced in the rearview mirror, searching for anything unusual. Odd things had been happening along I-95 lately—random shootings, mysterious accidents, cars found with the passengers murdered.

The mobster wondered if a madman was loose on the highway.

Angelo's mouth started to water as soon as they began the approach to Savannah, the home of Gert's Roadside Diner. A fleet of trucks in the parking lot signaled the popularity of the place.

He guided the sedan into a reserved parking spot at the side of the diner, a testament to Pinolla's long association with the establishment. Gert, an imposing blonde who weighed about 250 pounds, greeted the pair like long-lost brothers and steered them to a window table where they could watch over their car.

The mafiosi emerged an hour later and headed toward the Chevy, only to be intercepted by two Hispanics.

"Excuse me, mister," one ventured, "have you got a pair of jumper cables?"

Angelo raked his eyes over the pair while he chewed warily on a toothpick. There was no way he was opening the trunk with the unsavory-looking pair in the vicinity. "Do I look like a gas station? Beat it."

"Yeah, go on, scram," Rinaldo chimed in, moving up beside Angelo and reaching into his jacket for the butt of his pistol.

"Chill out, man, there's no harm in asking," one of the Hispanics said as they backed away, hands open and held at shoulder height.

The mafiosi relaxed slightly as the men turned to leave.

With the speed of a striking snake one of the pair spun, and Angelo caught a momentary flash of steel in the long-haired punk's hand.

Rinaldo clutched at his throat with a gasp of pain, blood flowing over the haft of a knife suddenly protruding from his neck. His knees buckled, and he sank to the ground.

Angelo stood rooted in horror for a long moment before reaching for his 9 mm pistol. A flying kick from the other mugger drove the breath from his lungs. He toppled, landing heavily as the gun slid from his fingers.

He felt a cold circle of steel press into the back of his neck. How did they know where to find us? was his last thought before his world exploded in a rush of searing pain.

1

Joey "The Fatman" Pinolla slammed down the phone, his ample proportions quivering in rage. "Franco, get in here," he shouted into his intercom.

Franco Garibaldi was the number two man in the Pinolla organization, underling to the don of one of the more successful of the Southern crime syndicates. Pinolla had gradually expanded his empire from its Miami base up the coast of the Eastern Seaboard until its many tentacles reached to the outskirts of New York. Although other crime Families controlled the main urban centers and large portions of rural America along the way, the Fatman had made himself useful—and successful—as the main distributor of cocaine and heroin along the I-95.

It was a profitable business he didn't intend to lose.

Garibaldi dropped into the chair across from Pinolla, bracing himself for a storm.

"I just got a call from Gert down near Savannah. Someone bushwhacked Angelo and Rinaldo, and took five million dollars' worth of my cocaine. Stuff that I had promised to our New York connection."

"That's tough." Franco shook his head in commiseration. "They were both good men."

Pinolla dismissed them with one chop of a pudgy hand. "After losing that much of my dope, they're better off dead. But that doesn't mean that we aren't going to avenge them. As soon as we find out who's behind this, we'll hit them hard."

Garibaldi nodded his agreement. That was the way the game was played. If someone hit you, you hit back harder until they got the message to leave Pinolla territory alone.

Someone else needed a lesson.

"It's your job to find out who was responsible," Pinolla commanded, stabbing a finger in Franco's direction.

"What if it was just a lucky shot?" the lieutenant wondered aloud. "Maybe another of those random killings that have been going down along the highway."

Pinolla shook his head. "No way. It was too pat, went down too smoothly. Besides, I'm not going to risk more coke on the wild chance that someone got lucky. Someone knew the exact timetable of the shipment, and you're going to find out who."

"Maybe there was a leak from the New York end. Maybe Gert set it up herself."

"Just check it out," the Fatman ordered, waving his hand airily in dismissal. "Quiz everyone even remotely connected with the shipment. Put the word out on the street that I'm looking for someone who just became rich. But my bet is on that South American bastard, Cordero. There were Hispanics involved, and that wise guy has been sniffing at my heels ever since his ugly face hit my town. Get on it."

Franco nodded and headed for the door.

Pinolla's voice halted him on the threshold. "Franco, if you even have the tiniest suspicion about someone, don't be too nice about asking the questions, okay?"

Garibaldi left, a grin etched across his face.

IN A GAS STATION near the exit to Darlington, not far from Florence, South Carolina, a short dark-haired man sat in a Howard Johnson's Motel, reading a newspaper. Although he looked relaxed, sitting over his third cup of coffee and his second piece of cherry pie, his eyes roved above the paper to observe every large rig that pulled in for a load of diesel fuel.

He'd spent more than an hour waiting, watching the fuel pumps like a lover waiting for a hot date.

A tanker truck pulled into the bays, the monster kind, towing a smaller version of itself behind. Danger signs decorated every side of the rig. The short man couldn't begin to guess how many gallons of gasoline the twin tanks held, but he knew it would be more than enough.

The driver of the big tanker pushed through the restaurant door to refill his thermos while his vehicle's fuel tanks were being filled.

The watcher dropped a few bills on the table and tossed down the paper, his waiting over.

He meandered to the tanker, glancing around casually. The station attendant was fussing over the fuel gauges and no one else was in sight.

Wandering over by the main tank, the short man pulled a metal device from his pocket and pushed a button on its underside. A small red light winked on. He reached under the tank, and the device grabbed on with a firm magnetic grip.

A final glance satisfied the guy that his maneuver had gone unnoticed. He hurried to his car, mission accomplished. The tanker truck had been heading south. He pulled the sedan into the onrushing traffic, speeding north as fast as he could.

MACK BOLAN WAS ENMESHED in traffic on his way back south from Washington. Hal Brognola's briefing had been alarming, and the Executioner marveled anew at how inhuman man could be to his fellows. Bolan was on his way to Miami to do whatever he could to help out the big Fed.

He turned on the radio and idly dialed past a few stations until he found a newscast. The announcer's grim tone grabbed Bolan's attention.

"North Carolina State Police have reported six more deaths along I-95. Two vacationing families were found shot to death south of Enfield. In a separate incident, an elderly Florida couple were found dead in their recreational vehicle near Lumberton. Police are investigating, but the name of those slain will be withheld pending the notification of next of kin. This brings the number of mysterious deaths along I-95 to nearly thirty within the past few weeks, although these are the first recorded within North Carolina. Further details at the hour. Turning to sports—"

Bolan twisted the dial. The latest murders were no surprise to the big man, just part of a chain of gruesome events unfolding along the interstate. The press had only grasped the tip of the iceberg so far. According to Brognola, a trickle of blood had been building into a wave of mass murder.

Bolan eased the car around a long, sweeping bend, edging the vehicle into the passing lane and picked up speed. He bore down on the traffic that clogged the artery, a dozen assorted cars and a large tanker truck hugging the right-hand lane.

The lines of cars slowed slightly as they passed the tanker, the drivers giving the huge truck a wide berth.

The warrior glanced into the rearview mirror, checking on a bus that was creeping up steadily behind him. His eyes jerked suddenly to the nightmare flash of an explosion, shining like a new sun in his eyes.

The oil tanker had been consumed by a roiling ball of flame, the fire shooting hundreds of feet into the dull, overcast sky.

Bolan wrenched the wheel to the left, steering for the grassy median between the north- and southbound traffic lanes, just as the concussion hit him.

The sedan bucked, threatening to roll as the force of the blast rocked the vehicle. Bolan fought the wheel, braking while he controlled a skid on the grass, still moist from a morning shower. The last thing he wanted was to slide into the northbound lane and be broadsided by the oncoming traffic.

Hot junk metal rained from the sky among gouts of flaming gasoline, dropping like napalm. Small grass fires blazed along the median. Bolan braked to a stop at last and stepped from the car to take stock of the situation.

The tanker had practically disappeared, leaving only a metal skeleton writhing among the flames. A Volkswagen that had been following too closely had flipped onto its roof and sat in a spreading pool of blazing gasoline.

Bolan knew there could be no survivors in the inferno, nor in ten other piles of twisted wreckage burning near the tanker.

Injured people staggered from several damaged cars, scrambling to outrun the river of burning gas that flowed toward them like lava.

The bus that had been behind Bolan was in serious trouble. It had cartwheeled onto its side from the concussion and lay like a dead elephant on the shoulder of the road. A finger of fire crept across the pavement, reaching out for the bus's fuel tank.

Traffic in the opposite lanes had ground to a stop as the curious gawked at the destruction.

Bolan charged toward the stricken bus, determined to help anyone still alive. He didn't waste his time appealing to other onlookers for help. They stared at the carnage like voyeurs at a peep show, content to remain safe and anonymous while someone else took the initiative.

The bus lay on its left side. As he approached the wreck a window popped and several young men climbed from the opening and jumped to the ground. They ignored Bolan and ran for the safety of the median.

The warrior chinned himself up onto the metal skin of the vehicle and looked in, searching for signs of movement. A glance over his shoulder told him the gasoline was spreading in a widening pool. He had little time before the fuel encircled the toppled bus.

Several bodies were visible in the interior. Cries and moans told him that a few people were still alive.

Bolan eased into the bus through the open window, his feet searching for a secure landing. A few female cries for help echoed through the interior.

A man stood up behind him at the end of the bus, his feet resting on the corpse of someone not as fortunate as he. Blood dripped from the injured man's face. He took one look at Bolan, pushed open a window at the rear and slipped through. Another survivor was already following his example, with no thought to helping the other victims.

Bolan turned his back on them and began to work his way forward. Fortunately the bus hadn't carried many passengers. The rear and center sections were nearly deserted, with most of the passengers clustered near the front.

The first person he encountered was a young woman who was buried under the remnants of two seats that had sheared from the floor. Silky black hair concealed her face. Bolan felt for a pulse but couldn't detect one.

The next seat held a heap of bodies. A middle-aged man with a day-old beard sat on top of the pile, clearly alive and in pain. A broken bone protruded through the skin of his thigh. "Get me out, will ya?" he pleaded.

Bolan pushed out the nearest window and grabbed the injured man under the arms. Ignoring the yell of pain, the warrior shoved the man out onto the side of the vehicle. Bolan followed the man outside.

The pool of liquid fire had crept to within a few dozen yards of the bus. He had maybe two minutes more before the coach ignited. Sirens wailed in the distance.

"Lower yourself over the side and start crawling," Bolan ordered. "I'll help you when I can."

"Are you crazy?" the wounded man shrilled. "I can barely move. You've gotta carry me away from here."

Bolan pointed to the flaming gas creeping toward the bus. "You don't have time to argue. Move."

The big man climbed back into the bus. From the cries he'd heard earlier, he knew that there was at least one more person alive inside.

He wasn't going to abandon any survivors to a fiery death.

Bolan checked the elderly couple lying where he'd found the man with the broken leg and confirmed that they'd been killed in the crash.

He pressed forward and found that a young woman with a small child and an elderly Hispanic woman were the only remaining survivors.

The young woman had suffered what appeared to be a broken arm. The child was unconscious and breathing, a bloody gash on his forehead. Bolan grabbed the girl around the waist and thrust her through a window. He passed the child to her and followed them out, seeing them safely to the ground.

The fire had crept close enough to flush his cheeks with heat and send acrid, choking tendrils of smoke down his parched throat.

Time was running out.

Bolan didn't waste any more precious seconds. He clambered back inside and groped his way to the elderly woman, who stared at him with beady black eyes. She told him in Spanish that her back was hurt and that he would have to carry her.

The big man picked her up with an effort, straining to keep his grasp on the overweight woman. Sweat beaded his forehead as he maneuvered her through the window and onto the exterior of the bus.

He stepped outside to find the vehicle ringed by fire and flames licking at its base. A few yards away the man with the broken leg was being carried to safety by rescuers. A couple of cars had stopped to try to aid the victims of the catastrophe.

The warrior hauled the woman into a fireman's carrying position and sat at the edge of the bus roof, his legs dangling above the shallow slick of fiery fuel.

He slid down the roof of the tipped-over vehicle and fought to keep his balance as he landed hard, the weight of the woman almost toppling him facefirst into the inferno. The hot flames licked at his pants and boots and he tottered.

Bolan gained his balance and ran, splashing through the gasoline, bolting toward the median.

Behind him, the fuel in the tanks reached the ignition point and the bus exploded, consuming the bodies of the victims left inside.

A blast of hot air buffeted Bolan as he set the woman on a grassy knoll. He looked around, seeing a highway turned into a battle zone where the casualties were restricted to the noncombatants.

He had no doubt that this destruction wasn't just the result of an accident. Some warped mind had foreseen the horror, death and terror that would result from an evil plan.

The Executioner was hot on the trail of someone eager to mete out pain and suffering. Bolan would soon be knocking at the madman's door, demanding payment—in blood.

2

The lights of emergency vehicles flashed as the wailing of sirens penetrated the smoke-blackened air.

Bolan decided that it was time to cut out. He had no wish for an encounter with the police. There were too many awkward questions that could be asked, too much to lose if his identity was discovered.

The big man slammed the car door shut and steered onto the shoulder of the opposite lane, guiding the vehicle around the many cars parked along the highway. Then he wove his way north, content to put some miles between himself and the disaster site before doubling back on another route to head south again.

He was bound for Miami, where he had thought that his mission would begin. But Bolan knew that he was already in the middle of the war zone. There was no way he could accept that the explosion of the tanker was simply an accident. Too many accidents had occurred along this stretch of road for him to believe this was anything but another planned attack.

A gang of killers in Miami plotted murder and mayhem. Bolan had learned of their existence only a few days earlier via an urgent message passed along to him from Hal Brognola. As soon as he could, Bolan had hopped the next flight to Washington. In hours he faced the powerful mandarin of the Justice Department.

The relationship between Brognola and Bolan stretched across the years, mostly through hard times. The Executioner had been a hunted man, a moving target with a price on his head set by the very men he worked to protect.

As a friend and confidant, the big Fed had always stuck by him, even though they sometimes clashed on opposite sides of the issue.

The two men had squared off over Brognola's desk, half-buried, as usual, under an avalanche of paperwork.

The Fed looked at Bolan with red-rimmed eyes sunk deep into his bloodhound face. "It's good to see you, Striker," Brognola said, before launching into his explanation of his appeal.

Bolan merely nodded in reply. He wasn't inclined to idle chitchat and knew that Brognola would want to get right to the matter at hand.

"We have a serious problem developing." Brognola paused while the words echoed in his head, sounding lame and hollow even as he watched a brief smile crease Bolan's lips.

The world was going to hell in a bucket and he was announcing a serious problem as though it were something new.

"Let me tell you how things stand along I-95—it's a bloody mess. I don't know if you're aware of it, but someone has been wreaking havoc along the highway for the past week."

Bolan nodded. "There have been an unusual number of car wrecks and traffic fatalities in the last while, more than twice the normal amount. I've heard that random killings have been reported in several states."

Brognola bolted from his chair and began to pace like a caged tiger. "That's the word we've been giving out. We want to avoid a public panic. But the truth is a lot grimmer than that. The fact is, most of those traffic deaths have been murders.''

"Is this another serial killer?'' Bolan speculated.

Brognola waved the possibility away with one beefy hand. "No way, Striker. Some of the murders took place almost simultaneously in widely scattered locations. One man couldn't be responsible. This has to be an organized conspiracy.''

Bolan frowned. "Any leads?''

"Not a damn one,'' Brognola growled. "We've checked the victims every which way and there's nothing to tie them together. There isn't any particular discrimination—old and young, white and black, male and female—our killers have gone for them all. None has been involved in organized crime to our knowledge.''

"Has any kind of pattern developed?'' Bolan turned the possibilities over in his mind. Was this a terrorist venture? Anarchist? Some group trying to make a name for itself, or just some bloodthirsty madmen?

"Whoever has been doing the killing has been indulging in a little robbery as well. But whether that's the primary reason or not we don't know. The only pattern we recognize is that the killer preys on the roadside turnoffs and picnic grounds that line I-95.''

"What about motive? If we assume that this is all planned, who could possibly gain from this kind of random butchery?'' Bolan was puzzled. He had reviewed his mental list of terrorists and killers, and the MO of this group didn't match anything he was familiar with.

"I've got an idea, Striker, even if it is a little farfetched.'' Brognola sat on the edge of his desk, his tired eyes gripping Bolan's.

The big man gave the Fed his full attention. He had learned long ago that Brognola was brilliant in his field, with an intuition that had an uncanny way of piercing through a mass of seemingly random facts to extract the one kernel of truth.

"I guess you've heard of the proposed task force that's supposed to combat interstate crime?"

Bolan nodded.

"The reasons for a special task force are clear. Once drugs get in this country they can be transported along I-95 all the way from Miami to New York. It's already known as the Cocaine Pipeline. There aren't any interstate checks, unlike the ports and airports."

"What do you expect?" Bolan commented. "The state highway patrols are stretched pretty thin to try to cover hundreds of miles of road twenty-four hours a day. Local police don't have jurisdiction on the interstates, so they can't ease the burden or participate in busts along the highway."

"I know it," Brognola said. "The DEA and state bureaus of investigation are so tied up in their own bureaucracy that they're rarely available except on those rare occasions when we know in advance of a major shipment."

"So, to combat these monumental problems, yet another task force is proposed." Bolan tried, but couldn't prevent a mocking tone from creeping into his voice.

Brognola looked pained at the response.

This was a sore point between the two men. Bolan had no patience with yet another enforcement agency. In his experience, organizations grew until the whole objective of fighting crime was lost beneath mounds of paperwork. After a short time, rules and regulations became more important than results, and administrators spent more energy currying favor with their bosses than taking the war to the streets. The paper pushers expanded until the office buildings swelled to bursting, while the hard-working field agents gradually were left out in the cold.

And when it was finally clear to everyone that the new agency was a failure, the response was always to form yet another commission or agency or task force.

In Bolan's opinion, the bureaucrats had never learned and never would. That was why he preferred to work on the outside, without getting stuck in the bureaucratic glue.

"Look, Striker, I'm not going to argue the right and wrong of this new task force. We've got to play by our own rules until the American people decide to change them. My point is that there might be someone who badly wants to put a halt to this task force."

Bolan was a little skeptical. In his experience the big-money drug people thought of the police forces as being a very minor annoyance. The occasional bust was no more than the cost of doing business to the multimillionaire kingpins who controlled the crime syndicates. If profits were down the drug lords would simply raise prices. There was always an abundance of willing buyers no matter what the pushers charged.

"As it is," Brognola continued, "several of the people responsible for putting this thing together have been having second thoughts. Maybe the timing isn't right, they say. Maybe we should concentrate more on the average kind of everyday crime, like these interstate murders. Maybe we don't need another agency, after all."

"So it looks like this latest project might be going down the drain."

"Right. And the only people that would benefit are the dealers moving their merchandise along the interstate."

The big man shifted forward in his seat. "It seems kind of farfetched to me, Hal. But I admit that I don't have anything better myself just now."

Brognola's phone buzzed, and he snatched up the receiver. "I thought I told you to hold my calls?"

He listened intently for a moment, his eyes widening in surprise. "Tell him to go ahead."

The big Fed dropped the receiver into the cradle and punched the button that activated the speakerphone. "Speak of the devil," he said. "This might be a break."

"Is this the Justice Department?" the caller asked.

"Go ahead," Brognola answered.

"I've got information on the highway killings," the voice said. Low and husky, it held a foreign flavor that Bolan placed as Latin American.

"It's the Fatman from Miami, Joey Pinolla. He's behind it all. He's the one you want. He's going to keep killing until you put a stop to him."

"How do you—"

There was a click, then the dial tone.

"Well, what do you think?"

"I've heard of the Fatman," Bolan replied. "He runs a Mafia operation in Miami, not that big. I never considered taking him on before. There were always more urgent problems to take care of."

Brognola tapped his desk with the end of a pen. "Something doesn't ring true, Striker. It's just too coincidental, too damned pat that we'd get a tip like this. And it doesn't explain why Pinolla would do something that would cause his organization to become the focus of a lot of heat."

"Yeah, you're right, Hal. There has to be more to it. Pinolla, like the rest of the Mafia dons, is a businessman. He's out for profit. Violence is just one of his methods. Where's the profit in random killings? I think he's being set up to take a fall for someone else's dirty work."

"You've probably hit the nail on the head. But it's the only lead we have."

"So what are we going to do about it, Hal?" Bolan already had a pretty good idea of what his friend would suggest. It didn't take a crystal ball to guess why Brognola had called Bolan to Washington.

"Striker, I don't think this department has the ability to put a stop to these highway killings—at least not any time soon. With a lot of digging around maybe we could assemble a case in a few weeks or months. If it's Pinolla, well, he's evaded everything more serious than a parking ticket for years now."

Bolan leaned back in his chair. "So you want me to find out what's going on and put a stop to it."

"If we wait for the wheels of justice, a lot more innocent lives will be lost."

The big man thought about it for a fraction of a second. This mission might require a little more government involvement than he normally liked, but the results would be worth it.

"Okay, Hal, I'm in."

THE ENFORCER STOOD for a moment in the phone booth after completing the call. It didn't make sense to Jorge to contact the cops and rat on someone, especially when Pinolla didn't have anything to do with the murders along I-95. Why did the boss insist on getting the Feds involved?

He didn't understand it, but the boss always said that Jorge wasn't paid to think, just to do what he was told.

That made him happy, Jorge thought as he climbed into his black Porsche. He had the cars and the women and no responsibility.

It was a wonderful life.

IN THE FEW HOURS that Bolan had spent in Washington he'd done some research in the Justice Department library.

The Pinolla Eamily controlled parts of several operations in Miami—loan-sharking, prostitution, gambling, and they had flexed tentative fingers into the drug trade. Lately it had been reported that they had gone legitimate in a big way, using crime money to buy up real estate and banking interests. Rumor had it that the former owners had agreed to very favorable terms in return for being allowed to live to spend the money.

Over the past few years there had been increasing pressure from the new boys in town, a Colombian organization now headed by a ruthless man named Jaime Cordero. Immensely rich as a result of the lucrative cocaine trade, Cordero had been slowly chipping away at the traditional Mafia empire.

Several times the rivalry had exploded into open warfare, littering Miami streets with the casualties of both sides. But lately an uneasy truce had developed.

If Bolan's hunch was right, the latest battle between the gangs was being fought along the I-95.

The big man had made a detour to Stony Man Farm, and the trunk of his rental car was crammed with the weapons of war he'd be using against the Mafia and Colombians.

Bolan hadn't started the war, but he intended to stop it cold—as cold as death.

3

Bolan arrived in Miami as dawn painted the sky a faint and delicate pink. He chose an inconspicuous roadside motel on the north side of town for a temporary base and hoped that his neighbors would leave him to sleep in peace.

Several hours later, as the sun climbed toward the zenith, Bolan awoke refreshed and ready to begin the hunt for his quarry. A few minutes later he was cruising along Biscayne Boulevard on a scouting expedition.

Brognola had given him a rundown on the major players in both the Pinolla and Cordero organizations as well as local hot spots where some of the cocky young hardguys liked to strut their stuff.

Bolan considered that the easiest way to eliminate the problem might be to simply destroy both organizations in a series of massive strikes. But there was no guarantee that he'd be shutting down the operation responsible for the highway killings by destroying the Miami organizations. It was too early in the game to eliminate the only lead that had turned up.

Until he could be certain he was on target, his objective would be to acquire the information that would allow him to eradicate the nest of vipers causing the carnage along the I-95.

The best way to ascertain that he was putting his finger in the right eye would be to penetrate one of the two groups.

Thanks to Brognola, he had a background that would withstand scrutiny. However, his terrific paper cover wouldn't be enough to get him through the front door of either gang unless he had a calling card, something that would bring him to the big bosses' attention.

Bolan had a pretty good idea where to get his ticket to the party.

His plan would have to wait for a few hours, until the people he was gunning for crawled out to make the rounds of their favorite watering holes. Until then, Bolan intended to make good use of his time.

He drove through Miami searching for the addresses imprinted on his file card memory, the headquarters of the rival gangs.

Joey Pinolla controlled his syndicate from a palatial mansion set on top of a hill with a magnificent view of Biscayne Bay. Gleaming two-story pillars fronted a home that smacked of an antebellum Virginia plantation. A fountain in the middle of a circular driveway cast wavering jets thirty feet in the air. Sculpted bushes framed the home, while palm trees waved invitingly. Uniformed men guarded a modest front gate. Both looked as though they belonged to a standard security firm.

They complemented the sedate, conservative appearance of the estate, as though Pinolla's home were the reward of a long and prosperous business career in something boring and drab, like shoes or cement.

Sure, Bolan thought, lead shoes and concrete coffins. There were probably a few undiscovered bodies at the bottom of the bay, courtesy of Joey Pinolla.

A few miles away, the Cordero gang gave a very different impression—a modern glass-and-concrete structure was perched at the edge of a cliff. A white Mercedes limousine crouched in the driveway, surrounded by flashy sports cars.

Several pairs of suspicious eyes watched Bolan closely as he slowed to take a long look while he drove past. The security staff ranged from blue-suited figures sweating by the front door, to assorted well-muscled hombres in jeans and T-shirts. All of them wore dark glasses, and every one looked meaner than a junkyard dog. Cordero didn't need a Keep Out sign to discourage intruders.

Pinolla's home looked like the kind of place where the society swells met for elegant charity functions, while the same people would probably cross the street to avoid walking in front of Cordero's.

Bolan guessed the Colombians weren't planning to win any good-citizen awards.

Appearances could be deceiving, but the warrior wouldn't give much for his chances of infiltrating Cordero's mob. He suspected that the Colombians would be very unreceptive to anyone who wasn't of their blood. Even if he made it in alive, he'd never be more than a bit player.

Anything he got from them would have to come from a soft probe, or through making someone talk by twisting his arm.

Bolan drove back to the motel to wait for darkness. He spent the long afternoon and evening checking his weapons, reading the background data on the crime families and planning his strategy.

The six-o'clock news broke the story of the highway killings in a small way. Some energetic reporter had put a few of the pieces together, probably with the help of a little green persuasion. Bolan watched images of the burning wrecks on I-95 while the announcer's voice-over recounted the path of destruction carved along the Eastern Seaboard from New York to Miami.

Bolan switched the television off. The stakes had been raised just a little. Every man who drove the highway would be wondering if the guy in the next lane was a cold-blooded killer, and probably packing a pistol in the glove compartment, just in case.

That sort of thinking caused accidents. Worse, it could turn a minor incident between two suspicious drivers into major murder.

Bolan checked his watch and decided that his quarry would probably be in place by now.

Brognola had agreed that Bolan's best bet would be to pass himself off as a former mercenary looking for a change of career. The government data banks held carefully planted files that would convince a curious snooper that Bolan had spent the years since the fall of Saigon kicking around the worst hellholes of Asia and Africa.

The warrior was going to sell himself as a dangerous, fearless and ruthless man. However, he was supposed to be an honest mercenary, meaning one who fought with loyalty and competence on whatever side purchased his services.

He could be a valuable commodity in a gang war.

Bolan dressed carefully in military fatigues, steel-toed boots and a black leather jacket. For this part of the mission he intended to conform to his cover. He strapped a combat knife to his right leg and stuck an assortment of garrotes, throwing knives and brass knuckles into his pockets. He wore a .44-caliber Desert Eagle in a holster beneath his arm. As a backup he packed the reliable Beretta 93-R.

Bolan drove into Miami, heading for one of the rougher parts of town. When he had passed through earlier in the day the streets had been a bedlam of small shops, crowds and noisy children. Now the shop windows were darkened, iron grilles pulled down over the store fronts for protection.

The only lighted fronts were late-night liquor stores and bars featuring exotic dancers. Drifters lay collapsed in doorways, while most corners held a quota of scantily clad and overpainted young women. A steady stream of cars cruised the avenue, occasionally slowing to examine the human merchandise on display.

Bolan parked outside a club called Chi Chi's. If his information was correct, one of Cordero's lieutenants, Hector Nuñez, liked to hang out here most nights, doing a little business and scoring with the local strippers.

He pushed through the outer door into a lounge scattered with small Arborite tables. A hard-driving rock beat pulsed from a sound system, not far from the lower end of the pain threshold. An amply built young woman crouched by the edge of a stage, her breasts hanging forward, as an elderly man stuffed a five-dollar bill past the elastic of her black panties. Cigarette smoke lay like a blanket over the tables, caught by the pulses of multicolored lights focused on the dancer.

Bolan drifted to the bar and ordered a beer. From his position he could examine the profiles of many of the other patrons. His back was exposed to anyone entering the club, but he had no fear of being recognized in this out-of-the-way dive.

The members of the audience were varied—old men and young laborers predominated. A scattering of men in business suits looked uncomfortable and out of place.

A few hookers sat by themselves, waiting to be approached.

Bolan picked up his glass and moved to the other end of the bar to change his viewing angle, since Nuñez was nowhere in sight. He gently shook off a slim feminine hand that reached for him as he passed.

The warrior reached the end of the bar and kept going. He'd spotted Nuñez sitting on the opposite side from the bar with his back tucked into the corner. The lieutenant wore an abundance of gold chains over an open-necked white shirt and an expensive suit. A muscle man sat beside him, clad in a chest-hugging black T-shirt.

Bolan approached warily, careful to keep his hands in plain sight. The enforcer's fists were below the table, probably holding a gun trained on the warrior.

The big man pulled out a chair and sat down without waiting for an invitation.

"Tell me why I should not kill you for being so rude?" Nuñez asked bluntly. His voice was flat and lifeless, but Bolan could sense the threatening tone.

"Because you're a businessman and I have something you need." Bolan lounged back in his chair, his eyes flickering from one Colombian to the other.

Nuñez exposed perfect white teeth in a feral grin. "What could I possibly want from you?"

"Protection," Bolan replied simply. "I'm the best bodyguard in the business. I can kill with any weapon or with bare hands. I can smell trouble a mile away. No one would even think of hassling you with me around."

"He doesn't need you," the hardman rumbled angrily. "He already has me."

Bolan grinned at Nuñez. "Look at that. A talking gorilla."

The tough guy glanced at his boss, enraged, begging for the chance to kill the interloper. The Colombian lieutenant shook his head slightly. "Let's take a short walk outside to the back of this establishment," he said to Bolan. "Then you can show me some of the talents you are so boastful about."

Bolan stood and let the other two precede him to the rear of the building. The Colombians paused at a door to gesture him through. The warrior stepped into an alley, a smelly hole lined with overturned trash cans and covered with broken glass. A wino got to his feet and staggered away as the open door spilled light into the lane.

The sound of metal rubbing on leather behind him made Bolan turn on his left foot and lash out with his right as he spun. His boot made contact in the center of the killer's chest, cracking a rib and driving it like a spear into the enforcer's heart.

The Colombian collapsed onto a pile of spilled garbage, blood pouring from his mouth. A revolver slipped from his grasp into a pile of wilted lettuce.

"What do you think, big guy, pretty impressive, huh?" Bolan addressed Nuñez with a mocking tone.

"Very," the drug dealer agreed in his flat voice. "I am sorry to lose Ernesto. He was very faithful. But just because you bested him does not mean that I will accept you in his place. Goodbye, gringo."

The lieutenant reached into his pocket and pulled out a Walther P-5. He sighted on Bolan and fired from the shoulder. But Bolan was already moving, and the gunman's shot missed.

The warrior dived to the ground and came up behind a shattered crate, the Desert Eagle a solid, familiar weight in his hand. One shot boomed like a cannon in the confines of the alley, and the top of Nuñez's head disappeared into the darkness.

Bolan walked down the alley toward the street. He had little fear that someone would report the gunshot immediately to the police. Whatever rough residents were on the street at this hour were no friends to the city cops. The urban jackals would be scavenging the bodies before Bolan was a block away if he left them in the lane.

He jogged to his car and backed it carefully down the lane until he reached the bodies. He levered them into the trunk.

Things had gone down pretty much as he had expected, although it had been worth a try. The Colombians were simply too distrustful of outsiders to allow one into the organization. However, his night's work had provided him with a bargaining chip that he intended to exploit.

Bolan drove the few miles that would take him to the gate of Pinolla's mansion. Three security men at the gate house demanded to know his business.

"I want to see Mr. Pinolla."

"I'm sorry, sir," the man in charge replied. "Mr. Pinolla doesn't see anyone without an appointment. Perhaps if you left a message and where you could be reached, one of Mr. Pinolla's associates could discuss the matter with you."

It was all very smooth, but Bolan noticed that the other two guards carried semiautomatic rifles pointed just away from the car. In a half second they could take him out in a deadly cross fire.

"Just call and tell him I'm delivering a present from Jaime Cordero. Tell him the present will spoil if he doesn't get it right away."

The head guard bit at his lip and went back inside the gate house. Bolan could see him talking into a phone, and later the gates opened.

"We will accompany you to the house," the guy said. He slid into the passenger seat. A second man positioned himself in back. Bolan could almost feel the rifle barrel pointed at the back of his head.

The Executioner drove slowly and was directed to a rear door. Several suited men poured from the house to surround the car, weapons in hand.

The big man climbed carefully from the vehicle, keeping his hands plainly in sight. The Mafia gunners would shoot him dead if given half a reason.

One of the well-dressed enforcers dismissed the guards and shoved Bolan roughly up the steps and through the door. Inside, he was searched carefully.

As the garrotes, knives and guns accumulated on a side table, the Mafia men grew restless. "This guy must think he's some kind of Rambo," Bolan heard one mutter.

"He's clean now, Franco," his examiner said, stepping back.

"All right, you," Garibaldi instructed, "follow me."

He led Bolan through several spacious and tastefully appointed rooms and stood outside an oak door. Someone in the Pinolla Family had a taste for fine antiques and muted pastels. Franco knocked softly.

"Come in."

Bolan stepped over the threshold and came face-to-face with Joey Pinolla. The Mafia don lived up to his nickname and then some. He overflowed his seat, covering the sturdy high-backed chair until almost nothing could be seen of the leather upholstery. A green banker's lamp shone over an immaculately clean desk, which was free of paperwork. Family pictures occupied one corner while a box of chocolates and a glass of bourbon beside a Jack Daniel's bottle sat on the opposite side.

Pinolla, heavily jowled and gray-haired, looked as harmless as an accountant, but the Executioner knew better than to be fooled by outward appearances.

"What's this?" Pinolla demanded, sizing Bolan up like a butcher examining a prime steer.

"He says that he's got a message for you from Cordero. All I know is that he carries enough hardware for me and five other guys."

"What's the message," Pinolla rumbled.

"It's in the trunk of my car," Bolan responded, imitating Pinolla's abrupt manner.

Pinolla motioned with his eyes and one of his aides disappeared to check out Bolan's car.

An uneasy silence fell in the study as Pinolla reached into a drawer for a file and began to read. Bolan glanced around, unimpressed by the rows of obviously unread books that lined two walls of the room. From what the warrior could see not a crack marred any of the spines.

The messenger came into the room looking slightly pale. "Boss," he said, "there's two stiffs in the trunk. One guy is Hector Nuñez, Cordero's number-one man. The other guy looks like muscle."

Pinolla threw down the document he held in his beefy hand and looked at Bolan sharply. "What the hell's going on?"

Bolan returned the stare with equal intensity. "Mr. Pinolla, I'm interested in offering you my services as a security consultant and bodyguard. I thought that my surprise would be a way to convince you I mean business."

"You don't need him," a tall broad man in a blue suit claimed. "You've got me."

"That's what the muscle man in the trunk said, too," Bolan taunted.

The enforcer shut his mouth abruptly.

"I've got lots of guys," Pinolla said, resting his chin on a plump hand. "Why do I need you?"

"It's not quantity, Mr. Pinolla," Bolan said with a grin. "It's the quality of what you've got. These guys don't even know how to search someone, let alone protect you properly."

"Says who?" one of the guards shouted.

"Check my belt," Bolan demanded.

One of the soldiers stepped forward and undid Bolan's black leather belt and pulled it free. From inside the belt he extracted a blade half an inch wide and six inches long. The razor-sharp metal was pliable enough to bend in half.

"I've got three other weapons on me that your men haven't found," Bolan announced, his eyes holding Pinolla.

The obese don was sitting back in his chair, hands clasped behind his head. Bolan knew he had the man hooked. Now it was a matter of reeling him in.

"Who the hell *are* you?" Pinolla asked.

Bolan shrugged. "I assume that you can check me out. I've built a reputation as a mercenary."

"And why have you come to me?"

"My last contract expired a while ago. I kind of got homesick for the States and American girls. A contact I met here told me there might be trouble between you and Cordero, so I thought it was worth a shot."

Pinolla leaned over the desk, impressed by the simplicity of the story, although his eyes never lost their cold, wary look. "So you killed two of Cordero's men just to talk to me?"

Bolan shrugged again. "I thought that I might see who had the best deal. They weren't very polite when they refused my services."

Pinolla smiled faintly, then his voice hardened. "There's one thing I want to know—will you be loyal or will you take my money and run at the first sign of trouble?"

"If I take your money I'll be as loyal as if I were your only son."

Pinolla sat back and contemplated the big man across from him. Something about the guy was intimidating, commanding. He wondered what the hell the man's game was. The merc was impressive, but Pinolla's suspicions wouldn't let him be lulled into trusting the man without some solid proof of exactly who he was.

The one thing the Fatman knew was that he'd rather have the guy working for him than against him.

"All right," he decided. "I'm going to give you a try. I can always use some strong loyal men. If you treat me straight you'll see that I can be very generous. If you cross me..." The don's small mouth thinned into a cruel line.

Bolan got the message.

"Franco, get him settled, then come back."

Bolan turned away, relieved that at least one part of the mission was out of the way.

"Hey," Pinolla snapped, "what's your name?"

"Jack Howard."

"I DON'T KNOW, Joey," Franco said, shaking his head. "Something about this guy seems a little off."

"Why?" Pinolla demanded, as he reached for another chocolate. "Just because he ices people who offend him? I can use a man like that. He certainly proved to me that my security could stand some improvement."

Garibaldi winced at the bite in his boss's tone. "Yeah. I screwed up. Sorry about that. It won't happen again."

"It had better not. Next time I might be dead, and if I'm dead, so are you." Pinolla searched his lieutenant's face. "But it won't come to that, will it, Franco? Because if I think you're slipping, I'll have you out of your job in a second. Is that clear?"

Franco nodded.

"Good. Now check this guy out thoroughly. Bring me a report in the morning."

The lieutenant stopped with his hand on the doorknob. "Joey, what if this guy's with the Feds or the DEA or something?"

Pinolla looked pained at the question.

"Use your head. Do you think that the government would let one of its agents run around the country knocking off the bad guys and stuffing their bodies into car trunks? Do I have to think for you now, too?" the Fatman bellowed.

Garibaldi turned on his heel without another word.

The don sipped his bourbon thoughtfully. Franco Garibaldi had been his right hand for nearly ten years. Maybe he'd reached his level of incompetence. Maybe it was time to put him out to pasture.

If this new guy was as impressive as he looked, maybe he'd found the key man he needed. If the mercenary was actually a plant from a rival gang, Franco would find out in short order. And the guy would quietly disappear.

4

Jaime Cordero scanned the *New York Times* for the results of his previous day's orders. His men had reported success up and down the interstate, but the drug lord was curious to see how it played in the newspapers.

There were stories of various killings along I-95 throughout the paper, with the greatest attention given to the victims of the tanker explosion. It had rated half a column on the front page, right below another garbage disposal story. Some of the killings had been connected, but it was obvious that much of the damage his men caused had been suppressed by the authorities.

That wasn't good enough for the Colombian. He dialed a Virginia number and fired off a set of instructions before replacing the receiver.

By afternoon a full description of the efforts of his loyal men along the interstate would be on the desk of every newspaper along the coast—without any means of identifying his organization, of course.

Within forty-eight hours there would be panic among the travelers of the highway, and the federal and state agencies would be falling all over themselves in their haste to calm the public.

Cordero studied a picture of the tanker wreckage on an inside page while a brief smile played over his lips. He savored the moment, feeling the satisfaction of knowing that with a single phone call he could cause terror to ripple through a quarter of the United States.

A knock on his door interrupted his pleasant reverie. A pale, nervous-looking face poked through the entrance. "Come in, Diego. I am not in a biting mood today."

Diego wasn't sure that the good humor would last. Cordero was known and feared for his rapid mood swings and volcanic temper.

"What is it, Diego?"

The underling paused while he tried to phrase his news in the least offensive way. As he looked at Cordero, Diego thought for the thousandth time how hard it was to believe that this young man, barely thirty, was soon to be one of the most powerful men in the Medellín cartel, the man responsible for the flow of more cocaine into America than any other person in the Colombian organization.

"It is about Hector," Diego said. "He and his guard were found in a trash bin on the other side of town. The police just phoned asking for someone to identify them."

Cordero punched in the number of a contact on the Miami police force. When the man answered, the drug lord questioned him rapidly and then went on hold while his informant checked the computer banks for information. Cordero tapped the surface of his desk rapidly with a gold pen, then grunted his thanks as his source passed along the data.

He strode to the window and looked out over the bay. Sunlight sparkled on the water and pleasure boats skimmed across its surface, but the view no longer gave him any pleasure.

"It appears that they were killed by a lone man who met them at a bar." He spoke quietly, as though he were conversing with the window. "There is no description of the man except that he was tall, dark-haired and Anglo. But I can guess who he works for. Pinolla!" he screamed, as he spun and swept the surface of his desk clean with one angry brush of his arm. Paper flew in a white blizzard; a ceramic lamp cracked in a hundred pieces against a bookcase.

"I want Pinolla to bleed for this," Cordero continued, breathing heavily. "Speak to me later. I am going to the morgue to identify the bodies."

BOLAN KNOCKED at the Fatman's door, flanked by two burly enforcers who stood a step outside of easy striking distance. For a fleeting moment he hoped that the powers-that-be back in Washington had, indeed, doctored his "file" enough to reflect the type of man he was pretending to be. If they hadn't, death would be swift.

The door jerked open and Bolan strode into the room, accompanied by his escort. The Fatman sat behind his desk, his chief lieutenant by his side.

"So, Mr. Howard, you think you're pretty tough, huh?" the Fatman asked without preamble.

Bolan merely nodded in reply.

The guard who had opened the door attacked without warning, driving a hamlike fist toward Bolan's right kidney.

The warrior sensed the attack; he'd expected some kind of test.

If Pinolla didn't kill him outright.

Bolan spun rapidly, catching the onrushing man by the wrist with his right arm, while a stiff left hand chopped downward. The guard dropped as though poleaxed, unconscious before he hit the floor.

The Executioner didn't wait for the other two mafiosi to attack. He knew that his agility and experience made him more than a match for any group in unarmed combat. He feinted to his left then right, lashing out with a steel-toed boot to catch one guy in the gut. As the injured man sank to his knees with the wind knocked out of him, Bolan kneed the enforcer in his outthrust chin. Number two was out of the fight.

The last guard, a huge, barrel-chested man with rock-like muscles in his forearms, charged, seeking to clasp Bolan in his outstretched arms and crush the breath out of him.

The warrior ducked low and pushed up, which sent the bruiser headfirst into a wall. The assailant crumpled into an untidy heap amid the wreckage of a lamp and an end table.

Bolan rotated his shoulders as he stood in front of the crime lord's desk again.

"Satisfied?" the warrior inquired.

Pinolla leaned back in his chair, noting that the big man in front of him wasn't even breathing hard after disposing of three of his top men.

There was a file folder on Pinolla's desk that Bolan guessed contained the background he and Brognola had decided on—that of a hard-nosed mercenary with a taste for excitement and the fast life.

"This file claims that you're an expert with almost every weapon made," Pinolla said, tapping the manila folder with an index finger. "Is that true?"

"I can handle anything from a strand of piano wire to an Abrams tank."

Pinolla's lieutenant interrupted angrily. "I think this guy is bogus, Joey. He's just bullshitting now. He's a phony."

Bolan listened with interest. Garibaldi was overreacting. Pinolla's man was obviously sorry that his confederates hadn't wiped the floor with Bolan. The warrior suspected he was feeling a little insecure after Bolan's performance. If so, the information could be used against him.

"Would you like to try me out?" Bolan replied. "I'll give you the choice of weapons."

"Yeah, come on, smartass. I'll cut your heart out!" the mafioso shouted in anger.

But Bolan noticed that he didn't make a move to come around the desk.

Pinolla held up his hand for silence. "There will be no fighting unless I order it. Now come with me."

The don heaved his bulk from the chair and pushed open a side door. The other two men followed. Bolan preceded Garibaldi, half expecting a sucker punch from him. But the capo knew the consequences of disobeying his boss.

They advanced into the middle of a large square room. Glass cases lined each wall from floor to ceiling, and museum cases were stacked in double rows along the floor. Each case contained either pistols or rifles, which ranged from antique flintlocks to state-of-the-art weapons that looked as if they had just come off the production line.

"You see my little hobby. I believe that I have one of the finest private collections in this country. A very American kind of hobby, wouldn't you say?"

Pinolla waved Bolan over to a wall that contained twentieth-century revolvers. "Let's test that knowledge you brag about. Tell me about that one," he demanded, pointing.

"It's the pistol version of the Uzi 9 mm submachine gun, engineered to fire single shots from a closed bolt."

"How about this one?"

"The Mauser HSc, introduced in 1938," Bolan replied easily. "The designation referred to hammer, self-cocking. It represented the best of German pocket pistol design."

"Very good indeed. One more, that one."

"Can I handle it?"

Pinolla opened the case and lovingly removed the gun. Bolan took it carefully and turned it over in his hands.

"A very unusual pistol," Bolan finally said as he replaced the weapon. "It's a 1935 Finnish Lahti pistol. An excellent cold weather pistol, very well sealed and provided with an accelerator. A bit heavy by modern standards."

Pinolla applauded softly. "I congratulate you on your knowledge and look forward to discussing armament with you some time. My other men understand nothing of the beauty of guns. But business presses."

The don turned and headed to his office. "Franco, you may leave. I said leave," he repeated as the assistant opened his mouth to protest.

"All right, Mr. Howard, you're hired."

"As head of security?"

"As a soldier." Pinolla smiled, but his eyes remained stone cold. "You might be more knowledgeable about guns than Franco, but he's family, my own first cousin. You're not family. At least not yet."

Bolan understood, but didn't much care. The warrior was content to be inside the organization. He didn't plan on sticking around long enough to become family, just until he had managed to fill the Mafia graveyard with another consignment of criminals.

JAIME CORDERO WAS in a rage. He had returned from the morgue after claiming the bodies of his men as the next of kin. He'd already arranged for them to be shipped back to Colombia for burial.

To many of his simpler-minded men, Cordero was a mass of contradictions. Most of them wouldn't understand why he had gone to the trouble of delivering the dead men to their families when he could have buried them in America.

To Cordero it was a basic case of loyalty. He expected loyalty, demanded it. For one of his men to betray him or defy him meant an ugly death by the drug lord's own hand.

He despised a traitor and would make an example of one.

But Cordero knew that the loyalty he demanded was a two-way street. Unless he was worthy of loyalty his men would betray him in his hour of need. For that reason he bought their loyalty with money, with women and with symbols that spoke on a deeper level. His men knew that he'd take care of them as long as they obeyed, even after their deaths, and the mothers of the dead men would receive a generous pension.

Cordero had never had the luxury of an education. He'd been too busy trying to survive on the streets of Medellín. The son of an illiterate street cleaner and a former whore, he had decided as a child that he would do anything to avoid the miserable life his parents had suffered.

When Cordero was an infant, his father had died of a fever and his mother had returned to the only trade she knew. She turned tricks in the bedroom next to his own until the night she was brutally murdered by a customer.

Later Jaime found out that the man who had murdered his mother was a Texan.

An American.

Left on his own, the youngster had drifted into the only source of wealth open to an ambitious but ignorant boy with no connections.

He had joined the drug cartels of Medellín.

Cordero had risen rapidly because he wasn't afraid of anything but failure. He'd accepted every assignment and triumphed as he slowly worked his way up in the organization, from street corner dealer to his present lofty position.

None of his men understood the reason why he'd ordered the murderous attacks along the interstate. To Cordero the reason was perfectly clear: his own survival was at stake.

The leaders of the Medellín cartel were men like himself. They had clawed their way to the top of one of the greatest criminal empires in the world, becoming billionaires in the process. Refined chemical death was their stock in trade, and damn the consequences to governments and people alike. Any kind of failure on Cordero's part would stop his climb to the zenith of power—and the kind of wealth and control that could topple nations.

The Colombian had particularly enjoyed his assignment in the United States. It amused him to see the people of this country—almost all of whom would have been rich by Colombian standards—fall prey to the poison he sold.

He laughed at the pathetic efforts of the police and the American government. They claimed to be waging a war on drugs, while underlings sold smack, crack, blow, snow, uppers, downers and a thousand other chemicals with impunity in the greatest cities and smallest towns.

Most of all it pleased him to see the rich capitalists clamor for the drugs he sold. At the same time the poor robbed the rich to support their habits. The United States was tearing itself apart in its eagerness to send billions of dollars to Colombia for a quick chemical high.

Cordero hated the United States. One of its citizens had killed the only person he had ever loved. Other than attaining great wealth, Cordero's goal in life was to crush America, in his own way.

He'd been given the mission of gaining control of the distribution of cocaine along the Eastern Seaboard as well as the wholesaling of the product. Profits would skyrocket to unimaginable heights if he managed to accomplish his goal.

To do so, he had to eliminate the main distribution network, which was controlled by the Pinolla Family. Then the way would be clear to eliminate the smaller organizations from Florida to Vermont. Soon every gram of cocaine sold in twenty states would be sold by his organization.

Then the powers in Medellín would accept him as an equal, and wealth beyond his dreams would be his.

It had been his own brilliant idea to create a diversion to occupy the attention of law-enforcement agencies along the route between Florida and New York. He had gambled that the tactic would prevent them from interfering when he made his move to take over the cocaine pipeline. So far it was paying off.

That he was able to bring pain and suffering to a few more Americans pleased him greatly. As a bonus, he might be able to con the authorities into helping him crush the Pinolla Family.

Cordero had no respect for the Mob. Once the Mafia had been strong and able, but too many years of living the American Dream had weakened the organization, making it vulnerable to an aggressive new force from Colombia.

Cordero and his men retained the nerve that Pinolla had lost long ago.

However, the Colombian was prepared to move cautiously. His rival still had great resources and a strong body of armed men willing to fight at their leader's command. Cordero acknowledged that the Mafia could still deal him a crippling blow before they inevitably succumbed to his own superior forces.

The phone rang, interrupting his train of thought. A light glowed on his panel, indicating that someone was calling on his private line, a number known only to a few people.

Cordero lifted the receiver to his ear and listened while he was given a series of rendezvous points. The crime boss dropped the phone and buzzed for his new lieutenant.

His temporary second-in-command was a man known as Snake, a reference to a large serpent tattooed along the length of his right arm. The man was a little old, often passed up for promotion because his vicious nature sometimes clouded his judgment. At the moment his normally flat, emotionless eyes glowed with eagerness to fulfill his new position.

"I have received word that a cocaine shipment will be passing through one of these points." Cordero handed over a list. "I want you to intercept it."

"Right away, boss." Snake turned for the door, clutching the list like a Christmas toy.

"Not so fast, Snake. I have something else for you. Here are the targets for the men along the highway. I want tomorrow to be the worst day in the history of the United States, a day that the whole nation will remember forever. After that is finished, I want everyone except those people I've listed to return to base. I might need them here for a very special project."

"Is that all?" Snake already looked as though he might be regretting his new assignment.

"Yes. This is one you will like. I want you to find whoever killed my men. Do whatever it takes to locate that bastard. And when you find him, bring him to me alive. Alive, do you hear? Then I'll show him what suffering means. I will flay him alive, an inch at a time until he begs for death. Now go."

Cordero turned to stare out over the ocean. It struck him how similar he was to the great body of water—relentless, merciless. And like the raging waters that sometimes ravaged the land, he intended to crush everything in his path.

5

Bolan awoke in a small room that he now called home. Located in a large outbuilding of the Pinolla mansion that served as a barracks, it contained a small washroom with a shower stall, a single bed that covered most of the floor space and a tiny chest of drawers. The only ornament in the room was a simple crucifix hung on the wall.

The previous night one of the hardguys had driven him to his motel to pick up his belongings. Bolan had packed up under the watchful eye of his chaperon. The warrior might have had a toehold inside the organization, but he still wasn't to be trusted.

A wise move on Pinolla's part.

On the other hand, his various weapons had been returned to him, although Garibaldi had cautioned him not to try to carry a weapon when he had an occasion to see Pinolla.

The Mafia lieutenant had also promised to shoot Bolan on the spot if he was so much as suspected of trying to pull a fast one. The grin on Garibaldi's face when he delivered this threat sent a not-too-subtle message loud and clear: the guy was aching for an opportunity to feed Bolan to the fish.

A heavy knock on the door caused the thin wood to shake. "Hey, you awake in there? Come on. We're leaving in ten minutes."

Bolan jerked the door open. A stocky, bald man, who was almost a foot shorter than the Executioner, filled the doorway. A cigarette hung from a corner of the older man's lips. "Yeah?" Bolan asked.

"I'm Silvio. I'm driving a load up north, and you're riding shotgun for me." The little fellow looked Bolan up and down carefully. "You'll do," he judged. "Get a move on. We don't have all day."

A few minutes later the pair were on the road, northbound in a nondescript sky-blue Oldsmobile. There was nothing about the vehicle to suggest that ten million dollars' worth of cocaine was hidden under the padding of the rear seat. But then that was the whole idea. No police officer would think to stop two law-abiding citizens driving an ordinary car. The vehicle wasn't so flashy as to attract attention, nor dilapidated enough to be noticed.

"This is a nice car," Silvio remarked as they made the turn onto I-95. "I'm gonna enjoy driving it."

"Do you get a new car each time?"

"Yeah. The boss has a chop shop across town. Some of the guys boost cars, take them into the shop and presto. A car with new numbers, different color and all that. The old owner would never know it was his. I can get you a great deal on a low mileage BMW, or any other kind of wheels you like."

"Sounds great. Where are we taking this heap?"

"You don't need to know, since I'm doing the driving. Just keep your eyes on the mirror and your finger on the trigger."

Twenty minutes of silence elapsed before the mobster spoke again, supposing that he had imposed his authority over his big companion.

"It's simple," Silvio explained. "We drive to Savannah, turn over the car to a new set of drivers and bring another car back to Miami. They'll change to local plates and another team will take it farther north. You'll be sleeping in your own bed tonight, kid. It's hard to believe you're getting paid for something as easy as sitting on your butt all day."

"If anything goes wrong, I'll earn my keep."

Silvio laughed, a high nasal bray. "If you don't, then we'll both be cashing in our chips."

Bolan reflected on the truth of his companion's comment as the car sped along the highway through the suburbs north of Miami. All it took was a second's inattention and he could be a dead man. One of the highway killers could drive up, take a bead on his head . . . and goodbye to war everlasting.

The warrior dismissed the thought, stifling a yawn. A lot of people had tried to remove him from the scene.

Bolan was still around.

His enemies weren't.

Hollywood and Fort Lauderdale vanished in their wake as he turned over the problem of where to go next with the mission. At the moment he was in the middle of a major drug smuggling operation with no way to tip off the authorities. He hated to allow a single gram of the deadly powder to slip through his fingers, let alone a couple of kilograms, knowing how it could ruin so many lives farther down the line.

He would have to wait for an opportunity to alert the police. If one didn't present itself, the warrior would have to destroy the shipment himself.

Bolan turned his mind back to the highway killings. He still lacked enough evidence to place the blame where it belonged. All he had were suspicions. "Aren't you afraid of the highway killers?'' he asked Silvio. "Don't you worry that someone might be planning to take you out the next time you pull off the highway?''

"No way. That last shipment of ours that got stolen, that was probably just a fluke. Too bad about Angelo and Rinaldo, though. I knew them both for years.''

"What happened to them?'' Bolan probed. This was information that wasn't in Brognola's dossier.

Silvio shook his head over their fate. "They were the two guys who got greased when someone robbed the Fatman of five million in snow a couple of days ago. Shot in the head, both of them. It was a real crime.''

Bolan assimilated the new information. It wasn't likely that Pinolla would be stealing his own narcotics or shooting his men. That pointed clearly to an outsider.

"Any idea who did it?''

The mafioso shook his head angrily. "I don't know. But if I didn't have a bad ticker," he said, thumping himself on the chest for emphasis, "I'd be on the streets twisting a few arms instead of sitting behind this wheel.''

"Is Pinolla doing anything about it?'' Bolan asked. "I mean, I don't know if I want to work for a guy who can't look after his own men.''

"You just hold on a second, buddy,'' Silvio retorted angrily. "Joey Pinolla looks after his own. He suspects it was Cordero, but he doesn't want a war without any proof.''

"He afraid of these Colombians or something?''

Silvio jerked the wheel as he turned toward Bolan, sending the car across the center line and earning a horn blast from an irate driver.

"Listen, Pinolla isn't afraid of anything. But Cordero supplies us with our cocaine and that's big business for us. Besides, we don't have as many soldiers as we'd like.

Just as soon as Pinolla is ready, you'll see some heavy hitting. So don't go mouthing off."

"Sure thing, Silvio." Bolan sat back in his seat, satisfied with the exchange.

If what the mobster said was true, someone was chewing at Pinolla's ass, possibly trying to swallow him in small bites. The Colombians were probably involved, playing a dirty double game against their Mafia clients.

It would take only a little more fire under the pot before the whole stinking brew would boil over to cause open war. Then it would be the Mafia against the Colombian upstarts.

They traveled the highway without incident until Silvio took a turnoff near Titusville. The little man wanted to stop for lunch at a place he was familiar with, a roadside topless bar where he swore none of the women was less than 38D. Bolan raised his eyebrows, but made no comment.

The warrior had kept his eyes on the mirrors during the trip. He wasn't as confident as Silvio that their shipment wouldn't be hit. Even to a large-scale dealer like Cordero, ten million dollars' worth of cocaine made a pretty sizable target if he was out to hurt the Miami Mafia.

Silvio spotted the diner about five hundred yards ahead and sped up. Bolan was more concerned with a small blue panel van and a sedan that appeared in his side mirror. They had come from the driveway of one of the homes lining the access road and were following a few car lengths behind.

"Silvio, when you get to the diner, I want you to drive right through without stopping, okay?"

"Are you crazy? I'm hungry."

"We're being followed."

The mobster shot him a glance filled with terror. Bolan guessed that the older man had been away from the line of fire for so long that he'd lost his taste for gunsmoke.

The restaurant was a large single-story building surrounded by a parking lot that was about one-third full. The wheelman turned in and kept rolling slowly as though he were looking for a parking spot. The van and sedan were right behind them. Bolan could now tell that there were at least four men on the hit team. They had probably planned to flank the Olds and hit them from both sides.

As the car neared the exit on the opposite side of the restaurant, the driver of the sedan knew that they'd been spotted. He gunned the car in an effort to pull it ahead of Bolan's Olds and block their escape. The passenger in the sedan drew a pistol, a wide grin splitting his face.

"Move it, Silvio!" Bolan shouted, drawing the Desert Eagle from its shoulder rigging.

Silvio spun the wheel and stepped on the accelerator, maneuvering the Oldsmobile just ahead of the pursuing car with a screech of tires. He then turned onto the two-lane highway that skirted the restaurant and pushed the gas pedal to the floor. The big engine roared and they shot down the highway.

The ambushers followed in hot pursuit. The sedan kept up and began to slowly close the distance, though the van fell back.

Silvio sped through a red light, narrowly missing a terrified-looking woman in a yellow Toyota. Fortunately the highway was nearly empty, although occasionally Silvio had to swing into the wrong lane to pass a slow-moving vehicle.

When the gap had narrowed to about a hundred yards along a straightaway, the gunner in the passenger seat of the sedan took careful aim out of his window with a rifle and got off several shots. Bolan thumbed down the power window and returned fire. With the speed of the two vehicles bouncing along the uneven asphalt, the warrior had little hope of a hit, although he hoped to keep the killers at a distance.

Bolan scored first, a round that cracked the sedan's windshield. The car dropped back.

Silvio suddenly uttered a strangled cry and clutched at his chest, letting go of the wheel. The Oldsmobile began to weave across the road as the older man slumped over the steering column. Bolan grabbed the wheel and jerked the vehicle into its proper lane. A car on the other side of the road drove onto the shoulder in a fountain of dirt in a frantic effort to avoid a head-on collision.

A quick glance at the old mobster told the warrior that he was dead from a heart attack brought on by the stress of the chase.

Bolan would have to think fast to avoid his own demise.

The warrior reached across and unlocked the driver's door, pushing it hard so that it would swing out. The Oldsmobile swerved into the oncoming traffic, barely missing a red Corvette. With a grinding roar of metal the sports car clipped the door and sent it spinning onto the road.

Bolan put his foot against Silvio's body and pushed it out the door. As the dead mafioso tumbled onto the highway Bolan slid into the vacant seat and groped for the accelerator.

The rear window dissolved, flooding the back seat with cubes of shattered glass. He glanced in the rearview and saw that his pursuers had closed to within a dozen yards.

A slug whistled by his ear and smashed through the front window.

A glance at the gas gauge revealed a steady drop—the fuel tank had been holed. He'd be out of gas in a couple of miles.

It was time for a few fast moves.

The Executioner wrenched the wheel hard right at the next intersection, fishtailing almost out of control as the wheels sought a grip on the rough surface of the road.

The Oldsmobile sped down the narrow side road as he scanned for a favorable place to make his stand. He watched in the rearview and saw that the van had come out of nowhere to make the turn. The sedan had overshot the turnoff, backed up and rejoined the chase.

Bolan slowed and veered off the road into a small stand of pine trees. He halted at the edge of the tree line and bolted from the car into the forest, slugs licking at his heels as a gunman in the van let loose with an automatic. Small branches drifted to the ground as the steady stream of rounds slammed into the pines.

The warrior dropped into a small hollow that was screened by saplings where he could cover the Oldsmobile. Bolan knew the car was the bait that would lure the bandits to their destruction.

The van screeched to a halt beside the disabled car. A gunner jumped out of the passenger seat. He laid down random fire along the edge of the tree line, trying to force Bolan to keep his head down, as he provided cover for the armed men who leaped through the side door and onto the ground.

But Bolan was already up and moving to gain a flank position on his vehicle. He was heavily outnumbered, and if he allowed himself to be pinned, he could be surrounded and targeted from several sides.

The warrior planned to even up the odds a little.

The machine gunner had paused and taken cover behind the van, possibly to change magazines. But from his new vantage point the Executioner could see three men who had jumped from the van working their way around the rear of the Oldsmobile.

He targeted the lead gunner and drilled a .44 round through his throat, drenching the Oldsmobile in a fountain of red. Bolan tracked his second shot in a heartbeat and took out a second man.

The remaining two men had prudently disappeared from sight. Bolan snaked away from his firing position in preparation for the reinforcements that would arrive in the sedan.

The vehicle pulled up farther away than he'd expected. Bolan shot a round at the passenger as the guy dived out the door. He thought he'd winged his target but couldn't be sure. The safest assumption the warrior could make was that both of the newest players were still in the game.

The hit men called back and forth to one another in Spanish. Bolan couldn't hear exactly what they were saying but braced himself for another rush. He rammed another clip into the Desert Eagle during the lull.

Machine guns suddenly belched fire, sending waves of death cascading through the forest above Bolan's head. The Colombians at both ends broke cover and zigzagged toward the trees.

Bolan squeezed off a round and one man dropped, his lungs sucking in blood and bone chips from his shattered chest. The other guy crossed the short distance into the woods before the Executioner could line him up.

The warrior faded back, the noise of return fire masking his almost silent withdrawal. He worked to his left on a course that he calculated would allow him to nail the hunter sent to get him.

Bolan was an expert in the art of silent movement and at making the most of every inch of cover. His opponent was an urban cowboy more used to whacking stoned addicts than dueling in a forest glade with a wary adversary.

The Colombian didn't know Bolan was near him until the last split second of consciousness, when a bullet from the Executioner's cannon crushed his ribs and exploded his heart.

Bolan began to run for the road as he heard a car door slam. The survivors had lost their will to fight and were preparing to retreat while they still could. As he reached the edge of the trees he saw the sedan screech off in a cloud of dust. The engine of the van had trouble turning in spite of the frantic efforts of the driver.

The vehicle sputtered to life as Bolan emerged from the trees. With a grinding of gears the Colombian backed onto the highway.

Bolan sprinted forward and jumped for the running board on the driver's side just as the van spun its nose to follow its fleeing companion. He steadied himself by grabbing on to the mirror. The Colombian's look of horror was erased by a point-blank shot to his forehead.

The warrior leaped down as the van slipped off the road and ground to a halt, the horn blaring to life as the dead man slumped over the wheel. Bolan jogged over to the vehicle, pulled the body from the driver's seat and laid it on the ground. He took a moment to wipe the bloodstains from the windshield, as he intended to use the vehicle and had no desire to attract attention.

He backed the van from the ditch and drove it the short distance to the disabled Oldsmobile, where he slit open the back seat and began to transfer the cocaine to the other vehicle. He paused to collect the wallets from two of the dead men.

Fortunately the van was unmarked and wouldn't appear out of the ordinary when he resumed the journey. However, he couldn't take the chance that some law-abiding citizen who witnessed the chase hadn't given a description of the van to the police. Bolan would have to ditch the vehicle at the first opportunity.

Bolan headed back to I-95 and continued north for a few miles. He then took a turn into a truck stop and found a pay phone. He needed to talk to Hal Brognola.

Without preamble, Bolan ran down the situation and what he had accomplished so far. "With what little I've seen, Hal, it looks like the Colombians are trying to pin the interstate killings on Pinolla."

"Sounds like it could play, Striker," Brognola agreed. "This morning I got another hot tip claiming that Pinolla's men were behind what's gone down so far. It looks like someone is trying to shut the Family down—with our help."

"How's the situation out there?"

"Grim. Someone's been shooting their mouth off to the press, complete with a package including a detailed list of all the incidents they claim have been perpetrated by the Mob. Stories have started popping up in the papers that there's some kind of terrorist conspiracy going on and that there've been a couple of dozen killings. People are panicking and screaming for every cop available to be assigned to I-95. The whole idea of a special task force has collapsed into name calling."

Bolan got an idea. Whoever was behind the highway murders had managed to destroy the possibility of cooperation between the various policing agencies. When the dust settled, even if there was a little more surveillance along the highway, the mobsters would still be left free to transport their deadly loads of drugs almost unopposed.

The Executioner intended to make sure that the fiendish little ploy exploded in the killers' faces.

Bolan changed the direction of the conversation. "I've got ten million in cocaine in the back of my van, Hal. If I can pinpoint the car carrying it north, can you make the bust without implicating me?"

Brognola thought the matter over for a few seconds. "Yeah, I think I can get it organized. Call me as soon as you know. But Striker, I want to warn you."

"What is it, Hal?"

"There's a lot of pressure to squash the Pinolla Family, even if we don't have any hard evidence that they're behind the butchering on I-95. I don't know how long I can hold off a move against them."

Bolan drew the implication. If the police came in he'd have to get out. He wouldn't risk placing himself in a situation where he'd be the target of the police forces. The warrior would never fire on a lawman carrying out his duty.

He gave Brognola the IDs of the two men whose wallets he'd grabbed. The man from Justice would run them down to confirm Bolan's suspicion that they were muscle for Jaime Cordero.

The warrior hung up and called Pinolla.

"What's wrong?" the Fatman demanded.

"Silvio's dead. We were hit on the highway. I still have the cocaine, but my car's gone and I'm riding around in a stolen van north of Titusville. What do you want me to do next?"

"Sil's dead?" Pinolla repeated, as though he were having trouble grasping this latest disaster.

"Yeah. A heart attack. I had to ditch the body."

Pinolla had pulled himself together. He gave Bolan the address of a garage in Daytona Beach where he could pick up another car to finish the trip to Savannah, and the location where he was to make the delivery.

"You make this delivery safely and there will be something worthwhile in it for you when you get back," Pinolla concluded.

"Thanks, Mr. Pinolla." Bolan hung up and drove the few miles to Daytona Beach, but he had a stop in mind before he made the delivery.

He pulled the van into an electronics store, and a few minutes later he was in the back of the van, slipping a bug into an open bag of cocaine. The receiver picked up the signal loud and clear. If the miniature tracking device performed according to specifications, Brognola's men should be able to track the cocaine from three hundred yards.

Bolan resealed the bag and went looking for a pay phone.

Brognola took down the information on the transmitter and promised to have men in position around the Savannah rendezvous by the time Bolan arrived. And the big Fed confirmed that the men Bolan had iced belonged to Cordero's organization.

Bolan hung up the phone feeling a measure of satisfaction, certain that progress was being made.

6

"What do you mean you failed?" Cordero almost shook in his rage.

"We intercepted the car just as you told us," a quavering voice replied over the telephone line. "Then we were spotted. So we ran it off the road and trapped the driver in the woods. The cocaine was just waiting to be grabbed. But that man was a killing machine. He shot the others. I barely escaped alive myself."

Cordero held the receiver away from his ear, staring at it as though not believing what he heard.

"Get back here as soon as possible," he finally said. "We will talk further."

The Colombian leader stood and began to pace. During the past few days, things hadn't been going according to plan. It was an unusual and very unpleasant feeling for Jaime Cordero to sense control slipping from his grasp. It took a real effort for the young man to even consider the possibility of failure.

Cordero summoned his lieutenant over the intercom. Snake arrived promptly and awaited orders.

"How many of our men have reported in?" Cordero inquired.

"Thirty-seven are here right now, and many more are expected by tonight."

The cocaine boss nodded his approval. "Good. Pick twenty and tell them there will be a mission later tonight or tomorrow. I will give the details of the strike later."

The underling left without comment. Cordero reflected that one advantage of having an assistant who wasn't too ambitious was that he wasn't inclined to second-guess his boss or bother him with tiresome suggestions.

The phone rang again. Cordero picked it up hesitantly, half expecting another dose of bad news. Instead it was his informant in the Pinolla camp.

"I have some information for you," the caller whispered. "Something that I am sure will be worth a bonus."

"Tell me and I will decide," Cordero barked. He was in no mood to play games.

"Well," the voice said with less assurance, "it's about that guy who greased your two men. Interested?"

"Go on."

"Well, he's here. He drove up to Pinolla's last night with your guys tagged and bagged in the trunk of his car. Pinolla hired him on as a soldier."

Pinolla! Cordero saw red at the mention of the Italian's name. He must be feeling brave indeed these days to antagonize Cordero in such a blatant manner.

"Why haven't you told me this before?"

"Hey, I was out of town. I just heard the scuttle when I got back. I haven't even seen the guy myself because the Fatman sent him up north with that dope shipment I told you about."

Cordero's head began to throb. A vein pulsed in his forehead as he made the connection between the events of yesterday and today. This one man, whoever he was, had become a murderous knife in his side, bleeding him of some of his best men.

"I want you to watch him carefully when he gets back," Cordero ordered in a barely controlled tone. "Let me know the instant you know he's outside Pinolla's compound. Is that clear?"

"Sure. But what about my bonus?"

"When that man is dead you will get a bonus that will make all of your trouble extremely worthwhile. I promise."

"All right. I'll call you when I have more information."

Cordero hung up and began to brood about how he would exact his revenge on this nameless foe.

BOLAN RETURNED to the Mafia stronghold just before nightfall, and Garibaldi was waiting to take him to the don.

"Tell me about what happened in Savannah," Pinolla began as soon as Bolan stood in front of him.

The warrior knew what was on the Fatman's mind but put a blank expression on his face. "Well, I drove the car I got in Daytona Beach to the address you gave me. Then they gave me a cup of coffee and a new car and I started back. That's it."

"What about the car carrying the cocaine? Did you see it leave?" Pinolla's lids were lowered, his voice soft and muffled, as though he were about to fall asleep in his chair.

Bolan shrugged. "When I left, the cocaine was still in the back of the van. What's this all about, anyway?"

"You expect us to believe that you didn't know the cops grabbed the coke outside of Savannah?" Garibaldi prodded.

"I don't expect much of anything from you," Bolan replied. He turned to Pinolla and continued. "This is the first I've heard of any trouble with the shipment after I left it in the care of your Georgia men."

"And what about Silvio?" Garibaldi attacked. "He's dead, you're here, and ten million of our blow is gone. I think you've got a lot of explaining to do."

"Yeah?" Bolan countered. "Well, why don't you explain how someone knew just where to hit us? Before he died Silvio told me you had been hit before I got here." Bolan looked Garibaldi directly in the eye. "It sounds to me as though you've got a mole around here, someone who knows enough about the operation to pass along information that someone else wants."

Garibaldi stiffened. "Are you accusing me of something?"

Pinolla broke up the argument. "Lay off him, Franco. I happen to think you did all right," he said to Bolan. "You kept the merchandise safe until it was out of your hands. I agree with you. There's something rotten in the Family. When I find out who has stabbed me in the back, he'll wish that he had been drowned at birth. Now go away, both of you."

His voice halted them at the door. "In case you were wondering," he said, his dark eyes boring into Bolan's, "I still trust you. Otherwise you'd be a dead man."

Pinolla watched the two men go. His composed exterior concealed his internal turmoil. The loss of the cocaine was serious. But even more important was that he was disappointing his customers. A few more losses and people would start to believe that he couldn't be relied on to deliver.

Once that happened his days were numbered.

Every two-bit punk along the East Coast would be biting at his heels. There would be pressure even from within his own organization to replace him with someone who could protect the Family.

Accidents happened, even to Mafia dons.

THE NEXT MORNING Garibaldi gave Bolan a new assignment. At noon he was to make a pickup of the morning receipts at a downtown collection depot housed in the back of a small trucking firm.

"It seems simple enough," Bolan commented, waiting for a reaction.

"Look, I'm tired of you already. Just keep your big mouth shut around me."

Bolan lunged for Garibaldi's arm. A second later the capo's face was pressed into the wall. The warrior jerked the guy's arm hard behind him, which produced a grunt of pain from his victim. "Listen, bozo. Don't play tough guy around me. I eat guys like you for breakfast. Understood?"

Garibaldi cursed in reply, and Bolan pulled the gangster's arm a little higher. "All right, I'll lay off."

Bolan dropped his arm and walked away without another word. He knew that Garibaldi wouldn't report the incident to Pinolla. The Fatman wouldn't want a security chief who couldn't control the troops.

The warrior didn't mind making an enemy of Garibaldi. When the inevitable final confrontation finally came, Bolan would benefit if Garibaldi's judgment was even slightly clouded by hatred of him. And in a struggle where the stakes were life and death, a man could always use an edge.

The altercation hadn't gone completely unnoticed. As Bolan walked away, an observer who had been dogging the big man's heels scurried the opposite way, searching for a phone.

AN HOUR LATER Bolan and another guard pulled into the parking lot of the trucking depot to make the collection. The real business of the firm was conducted in a small office well away from ringing phones and the distractions of loading docks and routing tickets.

The firm served as a convenient cover for the fleet of small trucks whose main business was making collections of protection money. Half the businesses in Miami sent payments through this office. Cash from gambling, loan-sharking and prostitution flowed into Pinolla's hands, carefully counted and recorded by several of the Fatman's most trusted accountants.

Bolan was to make the daily pickup and courier it to one of the local banks, where people didn't ask questions about large sums of money in small denominations.

From there, the warrior knew, the money disappeared down hundreds of different paths, both legitimate and criminal. Brognola had admitted to him that the Justice Department didn't have the time or the manpower to track down the crooked route the money took. Their investigators had never been able to prove wrongdoing or even tax evasion.

There was only one way to stop the flow of dirty money in Bolan's opinion: at the source.

The Executioner was just the plumber to fix the leak.

The warrior noticed that there were few troops, considering the amount of money involved. Three of Pinolla's men mounted permanent guard to supplement the security company personnel who manned the gates.

Pinolla wasn't exactly asking for trouble, but he did show some signs of being overconfident.

Bolan didn't plan to make the same mistake.

SNAKE HAD BEEN WATCHING the traffic passing through the gate with great interest, hoping that he and his men would soon get the chance to carry out the hit and get out of there. Two vehicles containing eight enforcers awaited his signal to begin the assault.

Snake smiled in anticipation when he recognized his target driving in. The boss's information had been right on the money. Cordero wanted this Mafia soldier taken alive for his amusement back at the fortress. Maybe it would go down that way, and maybe it wouldn't. He'd heard that this guy was pretty dangerous, and Snake wasn't about to risk his life so that the boss could get his jollies by torturing his victim.

Cordero's second-in-command watched his quarry walk through the door into the trucking yard. He picked up his radio mike and gave the signal for the assault to begin.

BOLAN STOOD in the doorway of the office scanning the freight yard. Behind him the other guards pushed a handcart that was loaded with bags of money that had been counted and locked. Today's take ran to nearly a quarter of a million dollars.

A squeal of tires announced that trouble was on the way. Two black sedans careered around the street corner and raced head-on for the gate. There was nothing to stop them other than the gate house, which was manned by two hired security men.

One of the guards moved into the center of the narrow lane, his hands raised to halt the speeding car. When the man realized that the uninvited gate-crashers weren't going to stop, he tried to jump out of the way. A fender clipped him and sent him sprawling, his leg a bloody ruin.

The second security man wasn't as lucky. An Uzi held by a passenger in the first sedan spit half a dozen rounds into the young man's chest as the vehicle roared by.

Bolan called out a warning to the Mafiosi behind him and unleathered the Desert Eagle. The big gun spoke once and the driver of the first car slumped over the wheel, his forehead missing. The vehicle continued on a short distance, then slammed to a stop against the cab of a tractor trailer.

The Executioner dropped another man as he climbed slowly from the wrecked car. The warrior dived for cover as a flurry of shots from the gunmen in the second car sang through the air.

The other four Mafia strongmen were in position and were peppering the invaders as best they could with their limited firepower, although two of them were dangerously exposed in the office doorway.

In a matter of moments the Colombians had improved the odds in their favor as they tracked a hail of submachine gunfire onto the two door guards. Both fell to the floor screaming, gutshot.

Bolan drilled one of the machine gunners who popped from behind his car to fire. A .44 slug carved through the killer's jaw, sending him flying backward in a spray of blood and broken teeth.

The warrior noticed that most of the heavy fire was directed at the remaining Mafia men. Two of the Colombians were following Bolan's every move with high-powered rifles, snapping off shots whenever he exposed himself.

Fortunately for Bolan, they weren't very good shots.

It made the Executioner wonder what the hell was going on and why he was being singled out for special treatment. But the big man didn't have a lot of time to speculate. He was too busy trying to dodge bullets.

Bolan decided to find a different angle of fire. He rolled to the left and came up running. Rifle rounds chipped concrete at his heels as he dived for cover behind a forklift.

The Executioner snapped off two quick rounds. Both riflemen paid the price of failure as the .44 Magnum blew away their lives with messy head shots.

The three surviving Colombians trained their machine guns on Bolan, the slugs rattling off the sides of the forklift.

The warrior crept into the driver's seat and twisted the ignition key. When the machine began to roll he directed it toward the Colombians' car, where the hitmen were sheltered. A pallet of crates hoisted in front of the forklift protected Bolan from the bulk of the attackers' fire.

The diesel bellowed as the forklift powered across the yard on a collision course with the vehicle. One of the Colombians trotted from behind the sedan to get a clear shot at Bolan. The submachine gun spit a staccato stream of death as the guy closed on the Executioner, firing from the hip. Wood chips flew from the crates and the metal body of the lift spanged with the tiny hammer blows of the bullets.

One shot was all the Executioner needed to eliminate that threat, punching a heavy lead fist through the assassin's chest as soon as the killer was in view. Bolan jumped clear just before the forklift thundered into the parked car. He dropped into a combat crouch, the Desert Eagle warm in his hand and nosing for targets.

A Colombian ran into view, his jacket flying behind him as he scampered for the gate, his weapon and mission abandoned. Bolan struck fast, sending the gunner tripping headfirst to the pavement with a blast between the shoulder blades.

The Executioner maneuvered around the car to check on his last quarry. The man lay spread-eagled behind the vehicle, his head out of view beneath the edge of a heavy crate dropped from the forklift. A small red puddle told Bolan that he wouldn't have to worry about danger from this quarter.

He glanced around the truck yard, which had been transformed into a killing ground in three minutes of fast and bloody action. The wail of approaching sirens announced that the police were finally on their way.

That marked Bolan's signal to leave. He holstered the Desert Eagle and stepped into the office over the corpses on the threshold to look for the back door.

SNAKE HEARD the police sirens as he sat nervously waiting for his men. The gunfire had stopped, and any moment he expected to see his men returning with the body of the man they'd been sent to capture, as well as the cash.

However, nothing was moving.

His view of the yard was partly obstructed by parked tractor trailers, but what he could see discouraged him. He could see four bodies of his own men, tossed like straw in a windstorm.

Trying to quell a sense of rising panic, the Colombian ordered his driver to move into the yard, then got out of the vehicle to look around. A quick tour confirmed his worst suspicions—all of his men were dead.

The lieutenant was covered in sweat as the car breezed along the highway back to Cordero's fortress. Snake tried to reassure himself over his failure. What was the worst that could happen?

Plenty, he realized with a sinking feeling.

7

"How come you're the only man left alive *again*?" Pinolla demanded.

Bolan stood in front of the Fatman's desk. Suspicion was heavy in the air. Garibaldi in particular seemed anxious to find a scapegoat.

"Men die when I'm around," Bolan replied. "I've made it my business to develop a talent for survival."

"I think…" Garibaldi began, but his voice trailed off as Bolan fixed him with a contemptuous look.

"Share your wisdom with us, Franco," Pinolla prompted in a sarcastic tone.

"I think something is fishy about all this."

"Brilliant. Now go about your business. I want to speak to Jack alone."

Garibaldi left, looking like a beaten dog. Even though he didn't know what he could have done to prevent the massacre earlier in the day, the second-in-command still felt responsible. Having the new guy stepping on his toes didn't make him feel any better.

The Fatman chewed on the end of a pen while he stared at Bolan. "Tell me again how everything went down."

The warrior described the assault step by step while the don stopped him every once in a while to question him further or to have him repeat a point.

"What do you make of the fact that two men with rifles were gunning specifically for you?" Pinolla asked.

"I think they wanted to take me alive and were shooting to disable."

Pinolla grunted and heaved his bulk from the chair. He paced over to a bar and poured a bourbon for himself, silently offering one to Bolan, who declined.

"I agree. But what does that mean?"

"That you have a mole. Someone is passing information to Cordero. Otherwise he wouldn't have known when and where to find me for the hit."

Pinolla raised his glass to Bolan in salutation. "Very good, my friend. And from your military training, what is the proper response?"

"You've been on the defensive so far. Now it's time to strike back. Hard." Bolan felt a little strange about giving advice to the Mob, but a seed of an idea was growing in his mind, a plan that could make the risky gamble of going underground with the Mafia pay off in a big way.

"What about the traitor?"

"You know your own organization. Who knew about both of the cocaine runs and the pickup this afternoon?"

Pinolla sank heavily into his chair and swirled his drink, tinkling ice breaking the silence.

"The only person I can think of is Franco. Others knew about one or two of those, but only he knew about them all. But I can't accept that one of my own relatives would betray me. Especially him."

"Then test him. Find out for sure."

"What do you suggest?" Pinolla inquired.

Bolan explained his plan.

A VERY DIFFERENT interview was taking place at Cordero's fortress.

Snake stammered through his report, glossing over the fact that he had only entered the truck depot long after the last shot had fallen silent.

Cordero stared at his subordinate in silence for a long while, and Snake tried to read his fate in the younger man's cold, cruel eyes.

"You have come back here, unwounded, with eight men dead and your mission a shambles?" Cordero's tone was flat and neutral.

Snake nodded as a drop of sweat trickled down his forehead and quivered on the tip of his nose.

"Take him to the aquarium," Cordero ordered the bulky bodyguards flanking the luckless Snake, "and assemble all the men except the perimeter guards."

Snake's eyes went wide in horror. He didn't begin to struggle until his wrists had been handcuffed behind his back. Then he began to thrash wildly and scream. "No, please!"

Cordero rose to follow. He paused to collect a memento from his desk—a switchblade sharpened to a razor keenness, one that he'd taken from the body of the very first man he ever killed. The Colombian had been fourteen, and the knife had stayed with him ever since as a kind of talisman.

It had a very practical side, as well.

The crime boss descended the steps leading to the private swimming pool in the basement. Not very large, designed for an intimate rendezvous. Cordero had converted it into a special attraction of his own, one that reminded him a little of home.

The small pool area was crowded, with his heavily armed men lining the edge of the kidney-shaped swimming pool, but not standing *too* close. At the far end Snake stood between his guards. Someone had slapped a large piece of tape over his mouth to muffle the screaming.

"Comrades," Cordero shouted. "Snake has been convicted by his incompetence. What is worse, I suspect that cowardice and gross negligence have led to the deaths of eight of our companions. I have judged him." He paused theatrically for effect.

"The sentence is death."

The crime boss walked slowly toward the condemned man. He drew the switchblade from his pocket and popped the blade. A third guard grabbed Snake's tattooed arm by the wrist, stretching out the limb.

Cordero slowly cut the sharp knife into the man's flesh. Snake writhed in agony, his muffled screams making the most hardened troops feel uneasy. In a few moments the strip of flesh that had held his mark was removed and held up for inspection. Blood ran on the tile and dripped into the pool.

The water thrashed as dozens of frenzied piranhas fought to taste the blood seeping into the pool.

Cordero tossed the strip of skin into the water. It rested on the surface for only a moment before disappearing in a tangle of gnashing jaws.

The crime boss nodded. Four of his henchmen grabbed Snake and swung him back and forth in an arc. On the count of three they flung him into the center of the pool.

The water reddened as the piranhas feasted on the victim of Cordero's brutal justice.

The rest of the troops watched in morbid fascination as Snake was slowly consumed. In half an hour nothing would be left but bones. It wasn't the first execution they had witnessed.

It wouldn't be the last.

BOLAN DROVE SLOWLY to his target, a Colombian distribution house that served as a reservoir for the street side dealers and small-scale pushers. The small-timers drifted back and forth all day, not willing to run the risk of being busted with a lot of inventory on them. They bought only enough to last for a few hours before making another trip to stock up again.

Bolan was going in alone. Garibaldi had been informed in private that the warrior would scout the area where they would strike and that Garibaldi and his hit team would back up the big man twenty minutes after Bolan started the probe. The lieutenant had been told not to say anything to anyone else.

If Garibaldi was the spy, then Cordero would have been tipped that he was coming. Colombian hardmen would be primed and ready.

If he made the hit without serious opposition, that didn't necessarily mean Garibaldi was off the hook, but it did lessen the chances that he was working for the other side.

It didn't matter either way to Bolan. The only thing he was concerned with was proving his "loyalty" to Pinolla and drawing the crime lord farther down the path to his own destruction.

Bolan drove slowly past the address he was about to hit, as though he were cruising the street corner pushers. The distribution house was a three-story red-brick building whose front was defaced with graffiti in a hundred shades. All the windows except for a single one on the side of the second floor were boarded over. Bolan noticed a dark face at the window and another on the roof inspecting the traffic on the side street.

One side of the building faced onto an empty lot that was covered with shattered brick and strewn with garbage. Customers came by and placed their cash in a paper cup suspended from a string. The distributors would reel in the cash then lower the coke or crack.

A similar dilapidated building functioning as a cheap flophouse flanked the target on the other side.

There were very few options for the warrior. He could either try to break through the front door or smash through a boarded-up window. Either assault would be spotted by the lookouts. He wasn't keen on being met by an angry reception committee.

He might attempt to march up to the front door as though he were a major buyer. The catch was that if Garibaldi had tipped off the Colombians, he'd be shot as soon as he stepped over the threshold.

Instead he'd enter by the only route left—the roof.

Pinolla had told him that there were usually two roof guards, who had a phone line to the interior as a warning system against police raids. Once approaching cops were spotted, the drug stash would go up in smoke.

Bolan parked his battered Mustang a few blocks from the drug warehouse and walked slowly back to the seedy hotel he had passed. The warrior was wearing a bulky black windbreaker to conceal the Beretta and Desert Eagle beneath.

A peeling placard at the front door advertised rates by the hour, day and week. As soon as he stepped inside, the smell hit Bolan like a wall. The stench of vomit, urine and unwashed bodies combined to produce an odor somewhat reminiscent of a stockyard on a hot summer day.

When an unshaven clerk in a dirty T-shirt yelled at Bolan to stop, the big man pulled out a fake gold detective shield, thoughtfully supplied by Pinolla. The sight was familiar enough in the run-down hovel for the clerk to return to his racing form without another word.

Bolan took the rickety stairs one at a time with the Beretta in hand, conscious that danger was a possibility in a place mostly filled with terminal losers and addicts desperate for their next fix. When he reached the top of the stairs he paused to screw a customized silencer onto the muzzle of the pistol. He didn't want shots attracting any unwelcome attention.

The door to the roof was old and rusty, looking as though it hadn't been opened since the building was built. Bolan shoved hard, but it wouldn't budge. He placed one foot against the opposite wall and his shoulder against the metal and pushed.

The hinges gave with a shriek, and the door opened about a foot and a half. Bolan squeezed through the gap, then switched the Beretta into 3-shot mode.

Two watchmen waited less than ten yards away on the opposite rooftop. One crouched by a telephone with his submachine gun beside him, while the other stood looking over the rear alley with an Ingram MAC-10 in hand. Bolan's unexpected appearance caused the Colombians to hesitate for a fraction of a second.

Which was long enough for the Executioner to swing up the Beretta and target a burst on the guy at the edge of the roof, blowing his brain to fragments before he had a chance to flip the safety on the Ingram. The gunner bounced against the parapet and toppled over the edge of the roof.

Bolan cursed as he swung the Beretta to acquire the new target. If the gangsters below spotted the falling body, he'd lose his edge.

The other lookout had gone for the phone instead of his gun. A trio of shots from the Beretta shattered the receiver in his hand. A second burst tumbled through the Colombian's chest.

The warrior measured the gap between the buildings with his eyes and judged it to be about fifteen feet. A two-foot parapet ringed each rooftop.

Bolan stepped quickly to the far end of the flophouse roof and sprinted, his powerful legs propelling him onto the parapet and out into space. For a fraction of a second he hung fifty feet above ground before his feet found the roof of the drug den.

He sprinted for the door that led into the interior, intent on making his sweep before the defense had time to respond or flee. He guessed that they'd first try to hit back, at least to buy themselves time to get rid of their stash.

The warrior descended carefully, checking for loose and creaking stairs as he went. Only a rare naked bulb illuminated the stairwell, leaving it cloaked in deep shadows. The upper floor of the building appeared deserted, although faint squeaks in the darkness told Bolan that more than one kind of rat had made this into a home.

Bolan froze as a faint clunk below him announced that someone was coming to check out the roof. The Executioner leveled his 93-R, targeting the turn of the stairs just below him.

A head appeared. The man was stepping cautiously. Bolan could have shot him just guided by the sound of heavy breathing. A second man followed two steps behind.

The Executioner was nearly invisible in the gloom, his black clothes merging into the darkness. He waited until the gunmen were both in plain sight, then he fired, catching the lead man in the throat. The dead man toppled backward into his companion as a trio of 9 mm slugs slammed into the second guy.

The two men rolled noisily to the bottom of the stairs. Bolan followed, watching his footing on the wobbly steps, which were now slick with blood.

At the top of the last flight, the warrior paused to insert a fresh magazine. Below he could hear shouting in Spanish. The surviving Colombians were fully alert now, and his advantage of surprise was gone.

He looked over the stairwell but saw no sign of the opposition. The area below was relatively clear, and he knew that if he simply barreled down the stairs there was a good chance a reception committee would be well prepared for his arrival.

Bolan examined the railing and judged it would take his weight. The big man decided to go for it.

He levered himself over the edge of the stairwell and crouched, holding on to the rungs with one hand. He dropped, pulling his feet under him and rolling with the impact. Bullets thudded dully into the plaster behind him and chipped grooves in the cracked and stained floorboards.

Bolan rose into a combat crouch and ran, snapping a burst low into the groin of a machine gunner. The Uzi flew out of his hands with a clatter, and the Colombian clutched at his leaking gut.

A slug tugged at Bolan's boot heel as he swept the Beretta to his left and targeted a pair of hoods firing from a doorway down the hall. Wood chips flew from the doorframe. A gunner screamed and dropped his gun, his hands clutching at his wounded eyes.

Bolan put him out of his misery with a perfect shot to his heart.

The last enforcer ran for Bolan in desperation, his machine gun waving wildly as he sprayed a stream of lead in Bolan's direction. The Executioner rewarded the attacker's bad aim with a shooting lesson, grouping three rounds on the bridge of the gunner's nose.

Scurrying feet behind him told Bolan that he hadn't cleared this nest of vipers completely. He spun to see a slim man with a gym bag clawing at the back door, fumbling with the bolt that secured it. The warrior thumbed the fire-selector lever into single-shot mode and squeezed a round through the back of the guy's head. He collapsed onto his gym bag, a large red blotch on the back door marking the spot of his passing.

All that remained now was to make sure Bolan hadn't left any enemies alive at his back. He glanced at his watch and noted that three minutes remained before Garibaldi and the backup were due to arrive.

Bolan checked the rooms by the front door first. He found them empty except for rusting beer cans, broken rotgut wine bottles and used syringes.

A small kitchen by the back door was in reasonably clean condition. A half-full percolator stood on a table, surrounded by cups of warm coffee and partly eaten muffins. Bolan noted the evidence of normal life, indications that the Colombians hadn't expected any trouble.

The room across the hall was where the actual inventory was held. A couple of boxes held nickel-and-dime bags of cocaine and a drum in a corner was partly full of doses of crack.

Bolan guessed the house contained a couple hundred thousand dollars' worth of drugs at the moment. Considering that this was only a tiny fraction of the chemicals that were reaching the street, it was easy to realize how much money was involved in the dirty business of drug trafficking.

The warrior sensed that he wasn't alone. A prickling at the back of his scalp informed his combat senses that someone else was nearby.

His eyes focused on a closet, its door pulled shut.

Bolan strode quietly to the closet and reached for the handle, his Beretta leveled in readiness.

The door flew open and a middle-aged man jumped out with a nail-studded board held over his head ready to strike down.

The Executioner stepped quickly to one side and pulled the trigger at the same instant, catching his assailant in the chest at point-blank range. The Colombian stumbled and crumpled to the floor, a wide exit wound in his back spilling blood onto a flowered shirt, mixing red into the pastel hues.

The big man moved to the front door, the rush of adrenaline slowly draining away. Now that he'd proved his loyalty, the challenges began all over again in a seemingly endless cycle.

Another step along the road of this mission accomplished, marked by the gravestones of a few more drug dealers. The former Colombian distribution house was now a slaughterhouse, the temporary resting place of a few criminals who would never ruin another life.

A small step in his never-ending war, but a step just the same.

Bolan cracked open the front door, watching for Garibaldi. Right on time two cars drew to a stop in front of the tenement, and men poured out of the sedans.

"Well, Garibaldi, I see you arrived just in time. All the fun's over."

Garibaldi flushed but decided not to make anything of it. He pushed past Bolan, his men at his heels.

Bolan could hear the mafiosi murmuring inside as they discovered the carnage and the stash of drugs. He wasn't listening. Holstering the Beretta he walked onto the street and toward his car. The warrior was already planning his next move.

8

Joey Pinolla was worried. The raid on the Cordero distribution house had been a success, but only a minor one.

The Colombians had lots of money, an ocean of cocaine and a seemingly endless supply of men imported illegally from the hills of their homeland. His own resources, although large, were by no means infinite. If he lost much more, particularly in trained manpower, he'd have to call in a few owed favors for some assistance.

Knowing some of the other sharks he had to deal with, even among the other Mafia Families, that might prove almost as costly as losing a war with the Colombians.

And a war it would be. Pinolla knew that he had raised the ante a little by striking back. With the Family to think of he'd been left without any choice. If the situation required negotiation some time in the future, Cordero and his ilk would only deal with a man of strength.

Any sign of weakness would be seized on—not only by the Colombians but by a hundred small-time thugs who would begin to think that maybe the Fatman wasn't so tough after all.

Pinolla had begun to circulate news of his raid on the Colombians through the criminal underground. Not only did he want that young upstart, Cordero, to know for sure who had knifed him in the gut—the don wanted everyone else to know as well.

That should keep the hyenas from nipping at his heels for a while.

In the meantime he had some business to take care of. Pinolla pressed the intercom and asked for the new guy. As Bolan stood beside the desk Pinolla looked him over once again, marveling at the strength and menace he exuded. Obviously he lived up to his appearance, since none of the men Pinolla had in his service could have done half of what he'd done so far and lived to tell about it.

This guy was something special.

"You did well earlier today," Pinolla said, reaching into a green gym bag that rested on the floor beside his chair.

Bolan recognized the bag as the one that had come from the raid. Dried red splotches marked where the dead Colombian had bled onto the fabric.

Pinolla pulled out a bundle of bills and tossed it to Bolan, who put the money into a pocket without examining it.

"Thanks."

"You keep up the fine job you've been doing and there will be plenty more. I told you that I reward loyalty."

"So you've decided that I'm loyal?" Bolan asked, arching a brow.

Pinolla waved the question away with a large hand. "I'm no fool. You can't expect me to just open my arms to anyone who comes through the gate. There are a lot of people who would like to see me dead, you know.

"Anyway, that's not what I wanted to talk to you about. What do you think about Franco?"

Bolan had debated what answer to give. If he claimed that Garibaldi was the mole, he'd have eliminated a key member of the Pinolla Family. That wasn't important. The warrior was more concerned with keeping Pinolla off balance. If the Fatman still thought that there was a worm in the apple, so much the better.

"I think he's clean," Bolan answered. "There was no sign that the Colombians expected me, and there were no more guards than I'd have expected."

Pinolla grunted in satisfaction. "I told you it wouldn't be Franco. I've known him as a straight guy for nearly thirty years, ever since we were kids together."

"What about a bug?" Bolan ventured.

"No way. I have the place swept twice a week."

"Then it has to be someone else."

Pinolla pounded a hamlike fist on the table. "When I find out who it is...." Suddenly he didn't look much like a jolly fat man.

The Mafia don opened a drawer, pulled out a slip of paper and handed it to Bolan. "Do you know them all?"

Bolan scanned the list. He'd spent his free time getting to know some of the other soldiers, learning their weaknesses, picking up odd bits of information. He knew that the six names on the paper were men high enough to have access to the kind of information useful to Cordero.

"Yeah. I know them all."

"One of them has to be the informer, or I don't have a clue who it is. You find out for sure."

"All right. Here's an idea. I told you before that I believe Cordero has singled me out for special attention. It's probably because I bagged two of his men. Just give me the addresses of six of your places around the city and call them to say someone is coming around for a security inspection."

"I understand what you're planning. I like it."

"Unless there's something else, I'm going to start baiting the trap."

"Yeah, there is one more thing." Pinolla paused and grabbed a couple of chocolates from a box beside the phone. "I want to know if you've got any friends like yourself who would be interested in making a good buck."

"I guess that depends on what they'd be doing."

Pinolla waved his hand impatiently. "The same thing you're doing. Security and things like that."

Bolan paused for a second while he examined the possibilities. He could use the opportunity to bring in a couple of FBI agents. He dismissed the idea as soon as it took shape. Having anyone else on board would be dangerous and would only complicate an already intricate game.

"Sorry. The only people I would recommend are already pretty busy in Asia and Africa—or dead."

Pinolla's face remained impassive, although Bolan could tell from a sudden contraction around his eyes that the Fatman was disappointed. Both of them knew that a war was coming and that Pinolla would have to gather additional forces to shore up his shrinking numbers.

"It doesn't matter," the don said blandly. "I just thought . . . well, get on with your plan."

Bolan left the spider spinning his web and began to prepare one of his own.

THE NEXT MORNING the Executioner set out alone to make the rounds he had scheduled. The day before he had spoken with each of the six men and had casually dropped the information that he was going to take care of some business of his own before he did an inspection the next day. Each man had been given a different place and time.

Bolan hadn't been able to detect anything definite from any of the suspects, although he had his eyes on one in particular.

The afternoon rounds went quickly as Bolan investigated a betting hall, a loan-sharking operation and a chop shop. He made careful mental notes that he would later pass on to Brognola for use by the Justice Department.

During each inspection he was only partly aware of what he was being told. Most of his attention was occupied with watching out for Colombian assassins.

One more inspection after dinner went without a hitch, so it was down to the last two possibilities: a brothel or an after-hours club. Bolan didn't want it to go down in either one, because if the Colombians chose one of those places for the hit, there was a good chance that innocent people would get killed.

He took some time out and phoned Washington, hoping to connect with Brognola at home.

"Striker," the man from Justice said. "I've been following your exploits from Miami police reports. It looks like you've been keeping busy."

"So far so good, Hal. I've been able to scratch a few players from both sides, although Cordero's and Pinolla's men are doing a lot to help me out."

"Whatever you've done, the problems along the I-95 have halted temporarily."

"I'm glad to hear it, but I'm working on solving the problem permanently."

"Striker, watch out. I've found out that the police or the FBI are going to try to slip someone into Pinolla's organization. They're under tremendous pressure from a few highly placed individuals. We're not getting cooperation, so I don't know how or when. They might already have done it. They're stonewalling me on this.''

Bolan gripped the receiver more tightly. As if his job wasn't hard enough already, now he was going to have to watch out for another operative without knowing whom to look for.

"Does this other person know about me?"

"No. You're definitely closed off. Look, Striker. I've got five minutes with the Man the day after tomorrow. He's the only one who can run interference for me. Until then, I don't know what to tell you. You're on your own.''

Bolan hung up. What else was new? "You're on your own" definitely had a familiar ring to it.

A few hours later Bolan stepped out of the after-hours club. The secret fun house was located above a hardware store in a commercial building indistinguishable from any of the others that lined the street. The club was a den where the bold, beautiful and stupid gathered to party. While a hot jazz combo played, the lawyers and accountants breaking out for a night on the town had been scoring some coke from Pinolla's men. The place had reeked of the heavy, sweet scent of marijuana.

Bolan sucked fresh air into his lungs gratefully, glad to be out of the hot and crowded room. He'd parked a couple of blocks away. Naturally Pinolla didn't want to advertise the club's existence with a parking lot full of cars in the midnight hours. Bolan didn't mind the walk. It gave him time to consider his next move.

His tour was over and there hadn't been a nibble. He guessed that he might as well give up the hunt for the spy. Maybe the mole suspected that Pinolla was on to him and had shut up until the hunt for him was over. The chances of catching the quarry were diminishing fast.

The warrior speculated that it might be time to take the action on the road and to crush both organizations from the outside.

Not yet, he told himself.

He had one more ploy that he was determined to try.

In the meantime he was content to abandon the fruitless chase and head back to the estate.

Bolan was suddenly aware that he was being followed.

A man had emerged from the shadows behind him and was trailing half a block behind. Bolan looked ahead and identified a second man, who appeared to be very interested in the empty window of a small jewelry store across from Bolan's car.

The Executioner knew he hadn't been tailed to the club. He was too experienced to have driven to the nightclub without spotting any kind of surveillance, and the bug detector in his car hadn't given an alarm. The two men must have been waiting for him to arrive.

The spy had revealed himself at the last minute.

The big man paused in front of an appliance store. Beyond the heavy metal grille a TV was broadcasting for insomniacs, featuring *The Munsters* in black-and-white. The man behind him stopped to light a cigarette and stare into the darkened storefront.

Now that Bolan was sure he was being tailed he had two choices: he could simply kill them both right now or let them close in a little and have them make the first move. He believed he wasn't in any immediate danger. Based on what he guessed of the Colombian leader's plans, their orders were to take him alive if at all possible.

Bolan moved on slowly, closing the gap between him and the man by his car. He reached into his pocket and grabbed a deadly surprise.

An engine coughed to life, and Bolan glanced over his shoulder to see a van approaching with its side door open.

The man in front of Bolan turned, a silenced pistol filling his left hand. White teeth flashed below a pencil mustache.

Bolan pulled his hands from his pockets slowly as though intending to raise them. Halfway up he flipped his wrist, and a razor-sharp throwing knife streaked toward the Colombian. The weapon flew true, unnoticed in the faint lamplight, until a sharp point buried itself in the kidnapper's heart.

The man pitched backward, dead before he hit the sidewalk. The Executioner dropped into a combat crouch, reaching into his jacket for the Desert Eagle.

The Colombian who had been behind him charged, snapping off single shots from a heavy-caliber pistol. A companion opened up from the van with an Ingram, spraying the doorway where Bolan crouched.

The warrior's hand cannon boomed, and the Colombian stumbled to the sidewalk, missing half a face. Bolan swung the pistol to intercept the van. A .44-caliber slug connected with the machine gunner, who tumbled into the street as lifeless as a rag doll.

As the van accelerated, the Executioner targeted the driver. The windshield shattered under the impact of the big slug, and the truck skidded out of control, pitching onto its side and tumbling upside down.

Bolan dashed for his car and gunned the engine. He shifted into gear and pulled into the street as flames from the broken van licked at the gas tank. As he watched in the rearview mirror, the vehicle erupted into a fireball. Anyone who had survived the crash wouldn't escape the flames.

The Executioner pulled into the street.

He smiled grimly at the mirror. The bait had been taken and the fish had been hooked. Now all that remained was to reel him in.

When Bolan arrived back at Pinolla's fortress, the boss was still awake, waiting for his report.

"So there's no doubt in your mind?" Pinolla asked when the warrior had finished. "Are you sure you weren't followed?"

Bolan shook his head. "To follow someone in a car properly takes half a dozen vehicles if the subject isn't suspicious. If he's wary and expecting trouble, it could take dozens of surveillance vehicles and highly trained professionals. I watched the traffic constantly and deliberately tried to shake anyone who might have followed. The only way the Colombians could have found me was to know in advance that I'd be at that club. And I only gave that location to one person."

Pinolla sat with his head in his hands, still unwilling to believe that he had actually been betrayed by someone close to him. "I've known Valerio for twenty years. All that time he's been my accountant. I treated him like my own brother. And now he's sold me out." Pinolla pounded a huge fist on his desk.

"I'll make sure that he wishes he'd never been born."

CORDERO STARED at the ringing telephone as though it were alive. It was the private line that only his bosses in Medellín used.

The drug czar dreaded the occasional calls from the Colombian headquarters. Sometimes it was a message that couldn't be trusted to regular communication channels.

Usually it was a warning—or a threat—when a leader was screwing up.

As he reached for the phone, Cordero comforted himself with the knowledge that he hadn't stepped over the line yet. If he had really screwed up, some of his own men would have burst through the door and killed him on the spot on direct orders from the cartel.

Cordero had helped remove ineffective leaders several times in his career, but had never imagined that he might find himself on the other end of an execution team.

He picked up the phone. "Hello."

"This is Rico."

Cordero's stomach lurched. Rico was the cartel's chief of dirty tricks. Political assassinations, executions of judges and witnesses who intended to testify against the cartel and internal discipline all fell under his control. The chief enforcer was a tiny man with washed-out gray eyes as cold as a storm-tossed sea.

Although Cordero suspected it was Rico who circulated a myriad of horror stories about his own brutality, the pocket-size killer made him very nervous. Cordero killed for a purpose—Rico simply enjoyed it.

"What do you want, Rico?" Cordero was aware that he spoke into a secure line. The same encryption devices used by the CIA protected the cartel's secrets. Enough money could buy almost anything. The drug lord knew that every word was being recorded in case the other members of the supreme command might care to listen.

Whatever happened, Cordero was too proud to beg.

"I have received disturbing reports about your latest venture. You lost four more men earlier this evening."

Cordero cursed under his breath. He knew there were spies among his people, who reported directly back to Medellín. It was wiser not to try to find them.

He just hadn't expected that they'd be so damned efficient.

"So far everything has been going according to plan. I have suffered some setbacks in the past few days, but even a great general cannot expect to win every battle."

"Be sure that you do not lose sight of the objective, if you wish to speak in military terms. I have been told that you have let an obsession with a certain member of the opposition blind you and color your judgment."

"There is one man who is responsible for everything that has happened to me. He is a devil sent to plague me. Once I have destroyed him, I do not expect any more problems."

"You are wrong, Jaime. *You* are responsible for everything. It is your plan. Make it work—or answer to me. See that you remember that."

The line went dead. Cordero had been given his one warning. He'd have to produce some successes bold enough to compensate for failure.

He was betting his life on it.

9

Bolan, Pinolla and Garibaldi stood outside Valerio Fraticelli's suburban home. It was three-thirty in the morning, and the moon rode high in a star-filled sky.

Pinolla's limousine and driver were at a twenty-four-
hour doughnut shop awaiting word that it was all over.

The Fatman rang the doorbell repeatedly, his fat
thumb jamming the buzzer. A light finally snapped on.
"Who the hell is down there?" a voice shouted from an
upper window.

"Me," Pinolla shouted.

A few seconds passed before a light beyond the main
door came on. Fingers fumbled at the lock.

Fraticelli opened the door, sleepy eyed and clad in an
overlarge bathrobe. He was a small man in his mid-
forties. The accountant lived alone, without even a
goldfish for a witness.

Bolan thought he looked scared, his guilt advertised on
his thin features. The traitor had probably been dread-
ing the knock in the middle of the night for as long as
he'd been betraying his employer.

As soon as the door opened Pinolla stepped across the
threshold. Without a word he cocked his fist and
rocketed it into the small man's nose.

Fraticelli sat down hard, blood streaming from his face and dripping over his pajamas and robe. "Why the hell did you do that?" he bleated.

"Tie him up." Garibaldi and Bolan picked up the accountant and carried him, shrieking, into the dining room. The lieutenant produced a coil of rope from a pocket and began to tie the prisoner to a chair.

Fraticelli looked from one man to the other, his fear of death lurking in his eyes.

"Look, Valerio," Pinolla said in a sorrowful tone. "It's over. We know you've been feeding stuff to Cordero. You just tell me what went wrong and maybe we can work something out."

Garibaldi squatted by Fraticelli and slowly removed a switchblade from his pocket. He popped the blade by the bound man's face and waved it in front of his eyes. "If you don't tell us every little bit you know, or if I suspect that you're holding back, I'm going to cut. And I'm going to keep cutting until I've squeezed every drop from your wimpy little body."

The point of the knife danced lightly across a corner of Fraticelli's eye. The small man tried to draw back his head, but the capo gripped him firmly by his sparse hair. Valerio opened his mouth, but looked too frightened to scream.

Garibaldi applied a bit of pressure on the blade, etching a small red line from cheek to chin.

Fraticelli fainted.

At a sign from Pinolla Bolan moved into the kitchen and returned with a pot of water. He threw it in Fraticelli's face, and the small man revived with a sputter.

"Now, Valerio, are you going to make me turn Garibaldi loose on you? I assure you it won't be pleasant, but you will talk. So save yourself all the unpleasantness, okay?''

Fraticelli took one more look at the knife and began to babble. Cordero had approached him a few months earlier, threatening to kill his mother and sisters unless he cooperated. At first it was just harmless bits of information, but soon the demands got heavier. By that time Valerio was already compromised. Cordero made it clear that he couldn't back out. One more week, Cordero had told him, and then he would take Valerio away and put him somewhere safe with a lot of money.

Pinolla sat silent for a moment. "I can't believe that you were smart enough to become an accountant," he said. "'Somewhere safe' probably means a pool of quicksand in the Everglades. Valerio, why didn't you come to me?"

The little man hung his head. "Cordero said he'd kill everyone in my family if I talked."

"You should have killed yourself instead, Fraticelli," Garibaldi mocked. "You know what happens to informers."

Each of them knew. By tradition Fraticelli would be handed over for punishment that would go on for days and weeks. Long before he died, Valerio would have gone insane from the pain, driven to the point where madness was the only escape from a universe with nothing in it but unbearable agony.

"That's right, Valerio," Pinolla echoed, continuing the good guy/bad guy routine. "Unless you tell me everything you know about Cordero's operations, I'll have no choice but to have you tortured. Otherwise, given the circumstances, I can cut you a little slack."

"You mean you won't kill me?" Valerio asked dubiously.

"Just talk. I'm not making any promises."

Valerio spilled his guts for half an hour into a tape recorder while Pinolla asked the questions. He'd been able to pick up tidbits of information, most of it of little use.

When he was finished, Pinolla turned to Garibaldi. "Ice him," he commanded.

"You're going to do me?" Valerio asked in surprise. "I thought you said—"

"You little bastard!" Pinolla raged. "Did you really think for a moment that I'd let you live after you stabbed me in the back? The moment I took my eye off you you'd probably run screaming to the FBI. No way. The only reason I'm not giving you to the turkey doctors is because I respect your mama. Now get him out of here, Garibaldi. If he gives you any trouble, bring him to the house and we'll arrange for him to go to the doctors. You hear me, Valerio? Now get him out of my sight." Pinolla pushed the beeper to summon his driver.

Garibaldi untied the informer from his chair and bound his hands before pushing him in the direction of the garage. In a minute he came back to get the keys to Valerio's car.

The garage door was opened and closed, and Garibaldi and Fraticelli set out on the one-way drive.

"Did you hear anything useful in there?" Pinolla asked, when he and Bolan were driving back to the mansion. The Mafia don had cracked open a bottle of bourbon. Pinolla had downed two drinks already, while Bolan was still sipping his first.

"Only that Cordero has started up a new crack factory somewhere near Boca Raton. I think he gave enough of a description for me to find it. If we tagged that, it would really hurt Cordero. Everything else was strictly small-time."

Pinolla grunted in agreement. "You up to leading a raid on it?" he asked after a moment. "If it goes well, you'll start moving up the organization fast. You've shown a lot of talent."

The Executioner grinned. "I haven't even begun to show you what I can do."

THE NEXT MORNING Bolan and four of Pinolla's henchmen made the drive up the coast to Boca Raton. He stashed his unwelcome escort in a motel near the beach and began to cruise in search of the target. All the warrior knew for sure from Fraticelli's information was that the crack factory was masquerading as a spare parts warehouse in an industrial park.

This made sense to Bolan. Other than a rare police patrol after dark, there would be little surveillance of the area. A bevy of small trucks coming and going—bringing in the raw cocaine and removing the processed crack—would look perfectly natural.

He stopped at a phone booth and ripped out the section of the Yellow Pages that listed various parts firms. After cross-referencing their locations with a street map, he at least had a rough idea of where to start.

Four hours later he was no further ahead. He'd examined each of the likely locations without striking pay dirt. As far as he could tell from a quick look, all the firms on his list appeared to be exactly what they claimed.

He was left with a choice between giving up the hunt or extracting the information from one of Cordero's men.

The Executioner wasn't a man to give up easily.

He was about to return to Miami when his attention was caught by a small blue panel van, the make that he'd seen Cordero's gunners driving before. The driver was long-haired and dark-complexioned, and could have been from a few dozen countries—including Colombia.

On a hunch Bolan decided to follow to see where he was led. Chances were that it would be another dead end, but he wouldn't be any worse off than he was at the moment. He eased the car into traffic and steered after the suspect, easily keeping a few cars between him and the van.

When the vehicle turned left onto a side street, Bolan had no choice but to tag along, even though he was completely visible to the other driver. The warrior dropped back until his quarry was a quarter mile ahead.

They had reached the edge of the industrial park before the van finally slowed and turned into a driveway belonging to a small isolated building. A garage door went up, and the van disappeared inside. As he drove by, Bolan noted that there were no signs that indicated what the building was used for. The structure looked like a flat box, devoid of features that would attract attention.

The warrior knew that the manufacture of crack was a simple process. When baking soda was added, cocaine rose like dough. After being baked to remove the water, it crystallized. The resulting crack was then broken into batches of about one-tenth of a gram. The baking process also removed many impurities, such as sugars, which were often present in cocaine. The crack that was produced was highly potent and was sold in small quantities.

From the producer's point of view, crack was a great product, since it sold for about double the price of pure cocaine. Easy to conceal and easy to sell, crack provided a quick and intense rush that left a desperate craving for more—and more.

Crack addicts were dependable customers and would eventually sell anything and everything they possessed, including their own bodies, to obtain the next hit.

Although the process was simple enough to be performed in an addict's kitchen, the high volume of business that Cordero's mob pushed made it sensible to take the manufacturing process somewhere a little quieter, a little more discreet.

Bolan figured the isolated building was an ideal location. Now he just had to prove his hunch was correct.

He pulled into a parking lot a mile down the road and turned the car around. On the drive back he inspected the terrain carefully, noting that the ground around the building had been leveled. There wasn't even a shrub within a hundred feet that could provide cover.

He also observed a number of video cameras posted around the edge of the roof, which were flanked by spotlights. The warrior guessed that the Colombians, if they were in there, wouldn't turn on all the lights unless they suspected someone was outside—a bank of blazing lights on a nondescript warehouse would be definitely suspicious.

He spotted only one door in front apart from a garage wide enough to fit two small trucks. There would probably be a second door in back, very likely locked and bolted.

There were only two ways in. He could either stage a frontal assault, say by driving a truck right through the garage door, or gain entry by stealth.

A frontal assault was always dangerous. The numbers fell fast, and bullets would be flying everywhere. As well, he couldn't be certain this was the right target.

If he took the quiet way he would be on his own—the noisy, untrained Mafia enforcers would prove more of a liability than an asset. Bolan phoned back to the motel and told the enforcers to keep out of sight until he called for them.

There were still six hours of daylight left. If Bolan was going to hit alone, he'd have to make use of whatever cover a night-time assault could provide.

Bolan had another idea that he wanted to try in the meantime. He drove back to the main road where he had first spotted the van and settled down to wait in the parking lot of a bathroom fixtures company.

A half hour later the blue van reappeared. Bolan eased out of the lot and followed in its wake, tracking it through the swell of traffic to a small beachfront property. A sleek power boat was tied up at the dock.

This could be a landing point for the Colombians. It would be easy for them to travel out beyond the three-mile limit in the boat and retrieve a cache of cocaine dropped off by associates.

Bolan circled the block and parked out of sight. He wore civilian clothes and was indistinguishable from the thousands of sun worshipers in the area, except for the light jacket that he wore to conceal the Beretta and Desert Eagle.

The house stood on a small knoll with the nearest neighbor a hundred yards away. Balconies on two levels looked over the ocean, while a five-foot stone fence surrounded the property.

Fortunately the approach to the fence was scattered with palm trees and shrubbery. Bolan covered the distance silently, flitting from tree to shrub with a practiced ease.

Standing by the fence, he was confident that he hadn't been spotted. He observed a man on the upper balcony with an Ingram MAC-10 in hand, staring down the beach with his binoculars at a small party of young women tanning in bikinis.

Bolan levered himself over the fence, dropped to the ground and stayed low in a combat crouch, listening. The sound of the ocean was all he heard. He had the advantage of surprise. No one would expect a bold attack by one man in the middle of the day.

Bolan unleathered the silenced Beretta and walked up to the front door, every muscle tense, every sense alert. He opened the front door, which emitted a raspy squeak.

A gunman walked into the hallway, and started in surprise when he saw the Executioner. Recovering, he swung his Uzi in Bolan's direction.

The Executioner fired first, punching a perfect round hole above the gunner's left eye. The guy toppled back, but his finger stroked the trigger reflexively as he died, sending a noisy stream of bullets chopping through the front room. The picture window facing the street shattered loudly.

The van driver rushed into the hall and fired a trio past Bolan's ear. The warrior replied carefully, targeting to wound instead of kill.

The driver dropped the pistol with a scream as a bullet carved through his forearm, shattering both bones. The guy sank to his knees, cradling his useless limb and shrieking in pain.

Pounding feet on the stairs announced the arrival of the other guard. His machine gun nosed for targets as he hurried to enter the fray. Bolan took a position where he could cover the stairs and watch the wounded man at the same time, in case he went for his gun.

The warrior dropped the watchman with a bullet above the ear before the burly Colombian even spotted the intruder.

The house was silent, except for the groans of the wounded man near the kitchen. Bolan stepped over the body of the machine gunner, who had tumbled to the foot of the stairs, and walked to the injured Colombian.

"Answer my questions and I might let you live."

The Colombian responded by yelling a string of foul curses and spitting at Bolan's feet.

"One last chance," the Executioner warned, sighting on the hardman's face.

"Go ahead and shoot! I will never tell."

"Wrong answer," Bolan said. The Beretta coughed once and the Colombian sprouted a third eye.

Bolan frisked the dead man and pocketed the keys to the van. He walked out to the vehicle and started the engine. Before driving off the big man searched the vehicle, discovering an electronic door opener and an Ingram MAC-10 with spare clips in the glove compartment.

The warrior believed that he'd found the secret to getting into the crack factory. He'd trigger the door and drive right in. He would take care of the rest of the details once he made it that far.

Twenty-five minutes later Bolan approached the warehouse. He turned into the parking lot and fingered the door control. The garage door rose, revealing a minivan with eight seats in the second parking spot.

The Executioner triggered the control as he drove through the opening and the door descended with a rattle, cutting him off from the outside. He jumped from the truck and focused the Beretta forward.

A pair of large sliding doors, both closed, led into the interior of the shop. A standard door beside them opened, and a sentry stepped in to check on the new arrival.

A question died on his lips as the Executioner drilled him through the heart with a 9 mm stinger from the silenced 93-R.

Bolan sprinted forward as the dying man collapsed to the floor in a heap. He holstered the Beretta and raised the MAC-10 as he ran, trading accuracy for firepower. He kicked open the interior door, his weapon tracking for prey. Rooted for a moment in the doorway, he took in the situation at a glance.

Then all hell broke loose as the Ingram began to bark.

Bolan targeted two guards who sat at a small table in the middle of the large room that was the factory. A flurry of .45-caliber rounds played over the killers, pulping the flesh of their faces and dealing their chests hammer blows. They pitched away from the table in a shower of blood and wood chips.

The Executioner shifted his attention to a duo standing by a row of ovens, supervising the baking of a batch of crack. He stitched a figure eight pattern of manglers from chin to groin. Their bodies danced a crazy polka, tugged by unseen strings.

The Ingram dragged up the last round in the magazine, and Bolan had to move. He dived for the shelter of a large drum of baking soda, dumping the empty clip as he moved.

The three surviving Colombians had recovered from the shock and were returning fire with a variety of small arms. Bullets pinged against the drum and flattened against the wall behind Bolan.

The Executioner rammed home a fresh clip and fired a burst in reply. The MAC-10 claimed another victim, punching the gunner into a tray of wrapped crack, which skidded across the floor.

The last two men decided to make a break. As one man laid down covering fire with a mini-Uzi, his partner streaked for the front door.

Bolan timed his moment well, poking the Ingram around the drum just as the Colombian reached the doorway and stitching a line of bullets up the guy's spine.

Now it had come down to a one-on-one battle. The first man to make a mistake would pay with his life.

The gunner had taken cover behind a floor safe and fired at Bolan sporadically with a 9 mm weapon that the warrior thought was a Heckler & Koch MP-5. The machine pistol was a deadly weapon with a 30-round magazine, but in Bolan's experience, a little hard to control one-handed.

The Executioner snapped a short burst, then laid the Ingram aside and unleathered the Desert Eagle. In a few seconds, while keeping a wary eye on the Colombian, he had removed the standard six-inch barrel and attached the fourteen-inch one in its place. The warrior always achieved remarkable accuracy with the long gun. He sighted on the edge of the safe and waited for the Colombian to reveal himself.

The gunman poked the Heckler & Koch around the corner, his head following it far enough for him to aim the pistol.

The .44 roared, and the Magnum round crashed through the enforcer's cheek and through the back of his skull.

Bolan holstered the gun. There was no need for a second shot. He rose to his feet and surveyed the killing ground. The encounter had produced eleven more cocaine-related deaths. Working in a crack factory was risky business.

Bolan noticed that the stoves were gas-operated. He opened the oven doors of all three, blew out the pilot lights and turned on the gas, then dragged one of the dead men near the open ovens. He pulled jackets off two of the corpses, rolled them into a ball and set them aflame. When the clothing was smoldering, Bolan made a hasty exit.

In five minutes he was parked down the road waiting for the explosion. He wasn't disappointed. The building blew minutes later, propelling the roof skyward in fragments on tongues of fire.

Bolan had wanted to send the message to Cordero that someone intended to reduce the drug czar's criminal empire to burning embers.

Starting now.

10

Jaime Cordero sat with his hands tented in front of his face, concentrating on mastering the panic that had begun to grow inside him. The latest news wasn't good. The loss of the crack factory and the distribution house had been more important in symbolic terms than in any monetary loss.

The Medellín cartel had a lock on the very profitable business of wholesale distribution to its many customers in the United States. Eighty percent of the coke sold in the U.S. belonged to the cartel, and the bulk of it flowed through Miami.

Cordero had wanted to show that he could control the whole cocaine chain, from the importing of the product in bulk right down to the distribution in small batches to the street-corner pushers. That required taking over the cocaine pipeline. If he had simply tried to set up his own network without eliminating the Mafia middlemen, he would have been asking for war.

He had simply decided to pick the time and place for the war himself.

Now his strategy had been dealt a savage blow. Every one of his men knew that he had been bested so far; his bosses in Medellín knew every detail of his every move. At any moment an execution team could burst through the door and put an end to the meteoric rise of Jaime Cordero.

The fear welled up again, but he pushed it down. If he was going to avoid a trip into his own deadly aquarium, he'd have to think fast and hard.

Cordero considered various options, calculating where Pinolla was weak and could be badly hurt. At this point the Colombian was willing to settle for a truce—provided it was on his terms. If he could force the Mafia don to give up his hold on the distribution along the pipeline, he would have gone a long way toward accomplishing his objective. There would be plenty of time later to crush the Fatman when he least expected it.

The Colombian flipped through the financial pages to give his mind a rest. Sometimes his best ideas came to him when he wasn't really trying to solve a problem. But it wouldn't work this time. Frustrated, he threw the paper into a wastepaper basket.

Something twigged as he stared out the window, recalling a small headline. He fished frantically among the refuse to retrieve the paper, tearing the pages in his haste. He paused, his long fingers tapping a one-inch announcement.

It was risky, but he knew that what he planned would make Pinolla come crawling.

Things were finally going to turn his way again.

"YOU SEEM TO ENJOY risking your life," Pinolla commented.

"Who dares, wins," Bolan responded, quoting the motto of the British SAS.

The two men sat in Pinolla's office, discussing Bolan's latest raid over a glass of bourbon. "I think we've won," Pinolla said. "After the latest licking you gave him, Cordero won't dare to mess with me or my boys again. Without Fraticelli to spy on me, he doesn't have a pipeline to information any longer. I've got his balls in my fist, and I'm squeezing real hard. I'm tempted to go in for the kill and kick his butt all the way back to Bogotá.''

Bolan discounted the Mafia don's bravado and broached the subject he'd been leading up to for days. "That's true. He's not as strong as he was a week ago, but he can still hurt you. You could lose a lot of men if he decided to go down fighting."

"Yeah, I could, but I don't think I will. I think that spider has had his nose bloodied so bad he'll hide if he so much as hears my name mentioned."

"All I'm saying is that maybe this is the time to think of ending the war and drawing up a treaty. You're on top, and Cordero's licking your boots. Tighten your grip and cover your backside."

Pinolla frowned and considered Bolan's idea. "I don't like it," he finally said. "Family blood has been spilled and I can't forgive that. I might want to keep the vendetta alive. I haven't decided."

Bolan didn't want to push. From what he knew of the pride of the Colombians, he didn't believe for an instant that the war was over.

There would be more blood spilled before long, and sooner or later the Executioner would maneuver Pinolla exactly where he wanted him.

The Fatman was headed for the killing ground.

SWEAT TRICKLED down Estevan's spine, making his shirt stick to his back. He glanced at Ricardo, his backup on this mission, and noted that the younger man displayed no trace of emotion.

Estevan reflected that perhaps he felt the pressure because this was his first major test in the organization.
Success in such a spectacular assignment could bring him
fame and advancement in the cartel.

Failure meant death.

Estevan had planned the strike the night before and
had reviewed it with Cordero until it seemed foolproof.
If it was as easy in reality as it had appeared in his boss's
office, in an hour he would be well rewarded and on his
way back to his beautiful homeland.

He and Ricardo were dressed in the livery of the
downtown hotel, and each man pushed a large trolley
loaded with the finest coffee and a mouth-watering assortment of muffins, rolls, cakes and fresh fruit. By
means of substantial bribes, Cordero had arranged for
the men who normally would have performed the service to call in sick. Estevan and Ricardo had miraculously been available to take their places.

The two were bound for a twenty-fifth-floor conference room, but had an unscheduled stop to make first.

Both men got off the elevator on the floor below and
pushed their carts to the maid station. Estevan remained
on guard outside while Ricardo took in the large covered
bowls of fresh fruit and dumped the contents among the
clean bedding and rolls of toilet paper. In its place he was
to substitute a pair of mini-Uzis and several spare 32-
round clips, which had been stashed in the closet earlier
by a confederate.

The unexpected occurred when a maid returned to the
station just as Ricardo closed the door behind him.

"Hey, what are you doing there? Are you stealing my
towels?"

"I wasn't doing anything," Estevan protested as the
woman pushed her cart closer.

Ricardo opened the door and handed out one of the silver bowls.

"What's going on? I'm going to call security about you two." She left her cart and started toward a house phone near the elevators.

Estevan glanced up and down the hall. Fortunately for him it was empty. As the woman passed he shot out a hand and pressed it over her mouth, cutting off a scream. He pulled the woman to him, and with his free hand plunged a long dagger up under the chin, slicing through the soft flesh.

As the woman went limp in his arms he opened the closet door and shoved her in on top of the fruit. He pulled dirty towels from her cart and hastily threw them over the body.

Ricardo checked Estevan's uniform for bloodstains, but the killing hadn't left any traces, other than a few small specks on the white gloves he wore to avoid leaving fingerprints.

Back in the elevator Estevan felt the tension drain, replaced with the restlessness of a soldier waiting for combat. With Cordero's guidance the Colombians had planned for a number of contingencies. Estevan had proved he could cope with an unexpected distraction. Now all that was left was to carry out the plan.

The door opened, and Estevan pushed his cart down the hall toward the conference room at the end, where the objective lay waiting. Ricardo followed, the tiny squeak of both carts' wheels and the rattle of cutlery resounding in the narrow hall. Ricardo moved up until the two carts were trundling down the hall side by side.

As expected, two men in dark suits flanked the double doors that opened into the room. Telltale bulges under the jackets marked the location of their pistols. Estevan knew he and Ricardo would be searched before being allowed into the conference room.

Both Colombians had a passion for knives, having spent long hours perfecting their skill until they could skewer the ace on a playing card from thirty feet. It was one of the reasons why Cordero had selected them for the mission.

When the two assassins reached the appointed place, a door fifteen feet from the guards, they drew throwing knives from their sleeves and let fly in one smooth motion.

Before the guards had time to react they were dead, each with a blade buried to the hilt in his chest. One man made a faint groan as he sank, but otherwise they died without giving warning to the men they had been protecting.

The Colombians dragged the dead men across the hall into another supplies cupboard, while anxiously peering down the hall for an unexpected intruder. This was the trickiest part of the mission as they had planned it, because if they were detected now the assassins might have to flee without inflicting any damage.

When the corpses were safely hidden, Estevan pushed open the conference room door and guided the cart through the opening. Inside, the room's lights had been dimmed, for someone at the far end was giving a presentation on an overhead projector.

Heads turned with interest as the Colombian entered, and a low murmur ran around the room, a sign that the busy executives called here today were as interested in their morning coffee break as they were in the presentation.

Two more guards stood at the back of the room. However, they looked bored and incurious, trusting that the pair outside would run interference with intruders.

The conference room was occupied by the directors of the holding company that represented Pinolla's main legitimate business interest. Thirty-eight men and two women were present, the presidents and chief executives of the financial firms that laundered the Mafia's illegal money into pure cash, spendable, taxable and totally legitimate.

Cordero had seen the notice of the meeting in the newspaper and had made his plans accordingly. The Colombian had seen an opportunity to make Pinolla suffer—and at little risk to himself—and he wasn't about to waste it.

Ricardo closed the door, and Estevan lifted the cover of the fruit dish. He gripped the mini-Uzi, keeping the lid between the gun and the guards.

The assassins dropped their pretense and opened fire, catching the Mafia security men first. Pandemonium reigned as the executives began to scream and dive for cover. They were trapped in the conference room, with the two killers barring the only exit.

The Colombians worked down each side of the long table, hosing the businessmen with a double stream of death. One brave man tried to charge with a chair in hand, but was stopped dead in his tracks by a 9 mm scythe that chopped his legs out from under him.

The Uzis chattered, playing an upbeat tempo as the Colombians waltzed the corporate wheels into the valley of death. They waved the machine guns like batons, orchestrating the shrill cries of the dying into a nighmare symphony.

Estevan felt a rush of excitement akin to pleasure as the blood flew, rejoicing in the slaughter of the fat-cat Americans. His smile broadened as he tracked onto the only woman on his side of the room, blowing off her designer glasses as she tried to hunch under the conference table.

Ricardo had emptied the chairs along his side and now crouched to pump a stream of manglers under the table, where the few survivors had taken refuge. He stood over the gray-haired chairman of the board, a man whose face appeared regularly in the business section of the city's newspapers. He obliterated the man's handsome features with one final burst.

It was time to leave the slaughterhouse. The police would be on the way.

The gunmen threw their weapons among the riddled corpses and closed the door as they left. Ten floors below a room held a change of clothes and phony identification. In five minutes they would be driving out of the underground garage to an executive jet fueled and ready for takeoff. In hours they would be in Colombia.

Estevan smiled happily. He had done great service to Cordero and the cartel. It had been the most memorable day of his life.

PINOLLA SAT IN SHOCK as a live television news broadcast showed an endless stream of sheet-draped bodies being loaded onto police ambulances.

The reporter confessed that there were no details available on the killers except that they might have been Hispanic. He then began to describe the massacre site in lurid and horrific detail for the third time.

Pinolla switched off the set. Thirty-six of the best people in his business organization were dead, and four more were in critical condition. Four of his soldiers had died as well. His financial companies would be in chaos for months, and the Fatman stood to lose millions of dollars.

The don reached for the intercom to summon Jack Howard. He paused with his finger on the buzzer as he realized how quickly he'd become dependent on the big man's advice and skill. It never entered his mind to call for Franco. His cousin just wasn't an ideas person.

Howard had been right when he said that Cordero wasn't finished yet. If he had listened to the big man's counsel, he'd have placed more security at the meeting, changed location at the last moment, maybe canceled it altogether until the trouble with the Colombians had blown over.

He should have listened.

The responsibility was entirely his.

The Fatman shrugged and pressed the buzzer. He needed help and didn't particularly care where it came from.

JAIME CORDERO WAS WATCHING the same broadcast in a much happier mood than his rival. The Colombian blew large smoke rings from his Cuban cigar at the screen, muttering a curse for the dead that he had learned as a youngster on the streets.

"I have hurt you, Pinolla," he said to the television. "When you come to me for mercy, you will think that I am giving it to you, but I will lie. You will suffer much more before I destroy you completely."

The Colombian had a tremendous advantage over his Mafia foe. For Cordero, men were simply a means to an end. They were as interchangeable as beans. For every man killed in his service, there were a hundred hungry, ruthless young men who were eager to risk their lives for a chance at wealth. He treated his men well only because it produced better results in the long term.

Pinolla was bound by the notion of family and had to be much more careful of his soldiers' lives. A loss of life in the Mafia was far more difficult to replace. Every death was a personal affair that sapped the morale as well as the strength of the organization.

Like a good chess player, Cordero was perfectly happy to trade meaningless pawns, knowing that he could afford to lose five men for each that Pinolla lost.

Cordero was deep in his mood of self-congratulation, when the door swung open behind him with a resounding thump.

The drug czar spun. No one was supposed to enter the office uninvited. Rico Guzman, the chief enforcer of the Medellín cartel, stood framed in the doorway.

"Good afternoon, Jaime. Are you not feeling well? You look pale. Or is it that you are not pleased to see me?"

11

"I want Cordero dead," Pinolla said flatly. "I don't care how you do it, just get to him and take him out. Scatter his brains all over Bay Front Park and run his headless body up the flagpole in front of city hall for all I care. Shoot him, blow him up or crush him like a bug. Just get the bastard."

Bolan privately agreed. The Colombian had moved the murderous private feud one step farther along the road of violence, taking the war to men and women who stood only on the periphery of the crime syndicate.

The executives who had been gunned down weren't lily-pure. They must have known that there was at least a hint of an underworld connection in their work. But even Bolan didn't believe they deserved a death sentence for their miniscule part in Pinolla's empire.

However, Bolan had to steer the Mafia don onto a road of the warrior's choosing. He'd worked hard to gain Pinolla's confidence, and now it was time to harvest the rewards of his deadly and unpleasant labor.

It was payback time.

"I know what you're saying," Bolan began, "and I appreciate why you want him dead. I do, too. I just don't think that blowing him away would be the safest thing you could do."

Pinolla swallowed a shot of bourbon. His cheeks grew red as he grimaced, making his eyes look small and beady in the folds of flesh. "What do you mean?"

"Say I try for Cordero and miss. What do you think he'll do then?"

"So don't miss."

"Easy to say. I've been lucky so far, but anything can happen. So what if he gets away?"

"You tell me. This is your story."

Bolan fixed the Fatman with a hard stare. "Cordero has already shown that he doesn't care who gets killed as long as it puts pressure on you. Anyone is fair game."

Pinolla's eyes widened as he grasped the significance of what Bolan was saying. "You don't mean—"

"I mean that if you push him, and maybe even if you don't, Cordero is likely to fight even dirtier. Wives, daughters, young children, parents, everyone connected with you and your men will be in the line of fire of the Colombian's assassins. He's immune. He has no family and doesn't give a damn about anybody. But he can hurt you badly if he decides to get personal."

Pinolla sat back heavily in his chair as though he'd been slugged. "So what can we do? I suppose you've got an idea?"

"We need a truce. You set up a meet between the two of you. Call in the dons of a couple of the other families to serve as mediators and get him to bring in a few people as well. Doing it that way saves face for both of you and makes it easier to work a deal."

The Fatman looked dubious. "I don't even think that I could sit in the same room with that greaseball without killing him, let alone negotiate a truce. Where's the honor in that?"

Bolan smiled sympathetically. "I agree. But there's nothing that says we have to keep a truce. The whole thing will be just a front. When we've lulled him into a false sense of security, we hit him with everything we've got. We could wipe out most of his organization at one time. If we kick the bastards hard enough, I think they'll look for fresh territory and leave us alone."

The warrior didn't actually believe the Colombians would give up on a money-making territory for a moment. They would likely keep trying to squeeze the Mafia out of the drug business until greater resources and utter ruthlessness finally won the battle. But it suited Bolan's purpose to play an optimistic tune for the Fatman. He only hoped the guy would buy it.

Pinolla looked at him speculatively. "Do you think that it would really work? Cordero is smart and experienced. Maybe he's too smart to fall into such an obvious trap. Maybe he'll try the same trick on me."

The don hadn't risen to his level of authority by being stupid and had been quick to see the flaw in Bolan's suggestion.

"You're right. Cordero might see it as a golden opportunity to wipe you out. He'll probably jump at the chance for a truce and plan to crush *you* when it suits him to try a double cross. But if you're smart and fast, you'll get him before he gets you. The better man will win, I suppose. But if you do decide to go with a temporary truce and negotiation, you can back out any time the vibes are bad and not lose anything."

Bolan sat back, wondering if he'd been a bit too obvious. He was pushing because he wanted the meet to take place. He just hoped he hadn't pushed too hard.

Pinolla was watching the warrior as though he were trying to read his underling's motives in his eyes.

Bolan wasn't giving anything away.

"All right, you've said your piece. Now I'm going to think about it, maybe find out what some of the rest of the Family think. Don't go too far—I might need you soon."

CORDERO SAT STIFFLY for a moment, then rose to greet his visitor. The thought ran through his brain that if he was marked for immediate death, Rico wouldn't have come himself. The savage Colombian had only to pick up the telephone to order Cordero's death.

"Rico, this is a surprise." Cordero moved slowly, careful to keep his hands away from drawers and jacket pockets. He was conscious that the little killer's massive bodyguard stood just inside the doorway, watching his every move suspiciously.

"I have come to assist you in dealing with your Mafia problem," Rico announced. "Although from the radio reports I understand that you have been making up for past failures."

Cordero mentally snorted at Rico's statement that he'd come to help. The cartel was giving him one last chance to prove himself. Rico was there to watch over his shoulder and drop the ax if he thought Cordero was incompetent.

Well, the little bugger would wait in vain, Cordero vowed.

Rico asked for a detailed explanation of the events of the past few days, and Cordero complied, emphasizing successes and passing off failures on the heads of dead subordinates. The drug czar knew that such explanations carried little weight with Rico, but Cordero would use every trick in the book to stay alive and invent a few of his own as he went along.

"In general, things have worked out as I planned," he concluded. "The interstate task force is dead, the cops in every eastern state are searching for serial killers, and the heat is going to fall on the Mafia. Once I have crushed Pinolla, the distribution network along I-95 will fall into our hands to our great benefit."

Rico sat unmoved and unimpressed. "Now that you have hurt Pinolla, how do you intend to finish him off? Surely you will strike while he is down, particularly since you have a spy on the inside to give you advance information."

Cordero shook his head, his cheeks flushing a little. "My source is no longer operative. I haven't heard from him in several days." He changed the topic quickly.

"Pinolla is weak but not stupid. He knows that I have the upper hand, in spite of his minor successes. He will seek to form a treaty to cut his losses. I will wait for him to do so and will not press him any further. Even an injured dog can be dangerous if cornered."

Rico drew his protruding lips into a pout under his thin mustache, signifying his disapproval. "Very well," he said. "It is your decision—and your responsibility." Clearly he would have preferred instant action.

"Show me your aquarium," he demanded abruptly, bringing the interview to a close.

Cordero led the way down the steps until the two men reached the pool. He stood directly beside Rico, topping the man by nearly a foot.

Rico wasn't having any part of Cordero's dominance game. The small man paced to the opposite side of the pool. "I must congratulate you on a very interesting and instructive method of execution. It is much more effective for your men to see someone punished in so graphic a manner, don't you think? If I was to conduct a demonstration, however, I think I would have the man lowered slowly feetfirst into the aquarium to stretch the demonstration out a bit." He stared at Cordero in a way that made it clear he wouldn't mind trying the experiment on him.

"It would only take about thirty seconds for the man to die after the fish bit through his femoral artery," Cordero responded, as though it were simply a theoretical discussion and not a personal warning.

"Ah, but what a thirty seconds that would be! I must think of having one of these built at home. For now, good day."

Cordero breathed a sigh of relief when his compatriot left. The little worm sent a shiver up his spine.

BOLAN WAS in the courtyard, practicing throwing knives at a target. An impressive collection of sharp blades clustered around the bull's-eye.

"I sure wouldn't want to have you mad at me," Pinolla commented as he waddled up to Bolan. "I just want to let you know that the meet is going ahead. I consulted a few people and they thought the idea of bushwhacking the Colombians was all right. I've invited Johnny Glisenti from Buffalo, Marcello Moscetto from Jersey and a couple of others from Philly, Chicago and New York. It'll give me a chance to introduce you to some of the boys. We've scheduled the meet for the day after tomorrow, if I can get that goddamned Colombian to agree. It also depends on whether we have a reasonable plan to whack the Colombians and keep our visitors safe. So tell me what you've planned."

"This is how it'll go down," Bolan answered. "The first day everything will go according to plan. That night I'll penetrate the meet site and plant some plastic explosives and a radio detonator. The next day you arrive a little late. While they are waiting for you, we trigger the bomb by remote control as you approach the meeting site. That's all she wrote. Simple, effective and with minimal risk to you and the others."

Pinolla rubbed his chin with the back of his hand. "How do you know they won't spot the bomb?"

"There's a type of plastique that I've used before that's odorless, stable and absolutely undetectable. A small amount will reduce a large building to rubble."

"I like it," Pinolla said, slapping Bolan on the arm. "If you need any help, just let me know."

Pinolla turned to go, and then stopped abruptly. "By the way, I want you to be in charge of security when we go to meet the Colombians. If they try anything, I want you beside me. You seem to have their number."

Bolan had to crush that idea in a hurry. "I don't think that would be such a good plan. I'd rather stay out of sight and observe the meeting place, decide how I'll get in and out. That sort of thing. Being tied down on a security detail might make that difficult. And my presence might antagonize Cordero. Garibaldi is a good man. He'll look after you and the two of you can brief me on the layout of the interior."

Pinolla hesitated. He'd come to regard Bolan almost as a good luck charm, but he could see the point of the argument. Reluctantly he agreed.

As the Fatman left, Bolan considered his plan, which was only a variation on the story he'd given the Mafia don. There would be a bomb all right, but the Executioner would make sure it destroyed both sides.

The important thing in the meantime was to keep out of the way of the arriving mobsters. He didn't know any of the men Pinolla had mentioned, but they might bring other men with them, old hands who could recognize Mack Bolan as the longtime number-one enemy of the Mob. Which wouldn't be good for his image as Pinolla's adviser, let alone his long-term health.

Using only a small part of his mind, Bolan drew another knife back past his ear and let fly. The larger part was laying out plans for the attack.

CORDERO WAS WORKING at his desk, reviewing the accounts of various satellite operations when the telephone buzzed. When he picked it up, his secretary informed him that Joey Pinolla was on the line.

Rico sat in a corner, reading a Spanish novel, doing nothing but annoying Cordero just by his presence. The younger man informed his superior of the call, and was told to switch on the speakerphone.

Cordero punched the button that connected him with Pinolla. "What do you want, Fatman? Have you called to beg for mercy?"

"Any more of your lip, Cordero, and I'll squash you like the bug that you are."

Cordero held his tongue for a moment, keeping in mind that his purpose was to draw the Fatman out, not to scare him away. "Go on, Pinolla, I'm listening."

"We're both businessmen. You've hurt me, but I've landed a couple of pretty good punches myself. This war isn't doing anything except making us fair game for some of the smaller outfits that would love to grab a piece of our action. I've called to arrange a truce and negotiations. I'm sure we can come to some arrangement that is mutually profitable."

Cordero smiled over at Rico with the knowledge that the mafioso was finally playing into his hands. After a few minutes of haggling, Cordero agreed to talk to his bosses about arranging a truce along the whole Eastern Seaboard.

When the call ended, Cordero turned to Rico with a smug grin. "I told you they would come to us."

His superior was skeptical. "How do you know it is not the Mafia who is trying to lead us into a trap? You could be setting us up for a disaster."

The younger man waved away his concerns. "We will strike hard and fast. Not the first day—they will be too suspicious. The second day when they arrive we will be waiting with weapons loaded. Not a man among them will survive. Think of it! They have given us an unprecedented opportunity to destroy not only Pinolla but some of the most powerful Mafia dons in the country. With them gone, we will be able to step into the vacuum and make ourselves masters of the drug trade in the whole of the eastern United States. At one blow we will extend our empire immeasurably."

Rico was only half-convinced. "I think that you are too enthusiastic, Jaime, too sure of yourself. The Mafia is not as stupid as you seem to believe—the dons will not be slaughtered like ignorant sheep."

"If I had told you last week that I would eliminate the cream of Pinolla's business empire, would you have believed me?"

Rico remained silent, unwilling to admit that Cordero had succeeded in a major coup.

"Besides, I am not saying that they are stupid, merely that we are more clever. Don't worry, Rico. Bring in as many of your favorite bully boys as you need to make you feel safe. Give me this chance for greatness for the good of the cartel. This opportunity will not arrive again soon."

The chief enforcer glared at Cordero, realizing that his subordinate's subtle dig at his courage had left him with only two choices. If he turned down the plan for the meeting, he'd have to kill Cordero right away. Otherwise, Cordero could spread the rumor that Rico was a coward. His other choice was to back the plan all the way.

Cordero stared back, knowing that he had backed the dangerous little snake into a corner. Would he bite or slither away?

"All right, Cordero," Rico finally said. "We will arrange the meeting. However, it must be at a place of our choosing, and I will look after the security personally. He has asked for at least two other representatives from the central committee, and I will arrange for that, as well."

Cordero reached for the phone to call Pinolla, but Rico stopped him, his voice low and harsh. "Just remember this, Jaime—any screwups and I'll see you writhing in your own aquarium while those snappers strip the flesh from your bones."

Cordero punched in the numbers of the telephone viciously. He wondered if he could somehow plan for an "accident" to kill Rico during the shoot-out with the Mafia.

That might be the only way to get the little shark off his back.

12

"I don't like this idea of meeting where that sneaky bastard Cordero suggested. I'm sorry that I let you talk me into it." Pinolla was dressed in black tie and tails, looking like a penguin with elephantiasis.

"We've been all over this. We let them pick the site to lull their suspicions. They won't ever suspect that we have sabotaged their own chosen meeting place." Bolan tried to reassure Pinolla, anxious to get him out of the house so that he could continue with his plan. The big man was dressed in a blacksuit, its multiple slit pockets holding special gear. The trunk of the car outside held camouflage paint and a pack with the plastic explosive.

"Are you sure you won't come?" Pinolla urged. "It's going to be a hell of a party. My friends are a real nice bunch of guys and I'd like you to meet them."

Bolan shook his head. There was no way he was getting into a room with an unknown number of mafiosi, several of whom might recognize him. "You go ahead and have a good time. I have a lot to do at the Colombian hideaway. There'll be plenty of time to party and meet your friends when we're dancing on Cordero's grave."

HOURS LATER, Bolan swayed with the breeze at the top of a small pine tree near the meeting site. Night-vision binoculars gave him a murky picture of the complex below. Still, it was clear enough to observe the watchmen making their rounds.

Bolan had spent the past two hours among the branches, and he was stiff with inaction. It was of the greatest importance to pinpoint the movements of the men below. This was to be a soft probe, a quiet penetration in which the warrior came and went as silently as a ghost.

The site chosen for the negotiations was a sprawling house set on several acres of suburban land. Part of the property enclosed one of the thousands of tiny lakes that dotted Florida. The building, from what Bolan could make out from his position, was a one-story affair surrounded by patios and gardens, and an Olympic-size pool sparkled in the moonlight between the house and the lake.

A six-foot wall surrounded the property and the only point of entry was through a single gate on the side opposite where Bolan nested like an owl.

The warrior had observed the guard patrols with great care. Two-man teams covered the wall in steady back-and-forth movements, passing about every three minutes. There was one roving Jeep that moved at random through the property, shining a powerful spotlight into the pools of shadows around the complex.

Lights burned in several windows, but Bolan believed that the house was deserted, or nearly so. He hadn't seen anyone eclipse the interior lights on this side since he had taken his observation post. An hour spent in a tree across from the gate had yielded little additional information, since the house was screened by foliage from that vantage point.

The warrior began to climb down. He had learned all he could gather from a passive observation from the outside.

Now it was time for action.

He was lightly equipped for the penetration. Since his intention was to avoid contact, he had brought a minimum of weaponry, trusting speed and stealth to bring him in and out of the target area.

The first barrier was the exterior wall. Bolan pressed himself against the brick and mortar, listening for the soft crunch of the guards' feet on the other side. The sentries passed beyond the wall with a murmur of low voices, the reek of their pungent cigarettes drifting over the wall.

Bolan waited an additional minute to allow himself to cross during the longest period between guard rounds. When the second hand crept to the appointed spot, he levered himself over the wall in one powerful pull.

He dropped to the ground, landing in a combat crouch. The nearest watchmen were a safe distance away. Bolan ran, keeping low to the ground until he reached cover behind a broad shrub. When no alarms were raised, he inched forward, keeping to the low bushes. Fortunately the moon was only a tiny crescent, bright enough to provide some additional visibility for Bolan, but not sufficient to reveal his presence.

The warrior's biggest worry was the possibility of passive devices scattered around the property. A motion detector or a hidden ground microphone could pinpoint the big man without his knowing that he'd been discovered.

There was no way to spot the devices or neutralize them without indicating that the security screen had been breached. Right now the Colombians could be preparing a vicious surprise for the moment he stepped from the shadows to approach the house.

Bolan froze as the patrol Jeep passed twenty feet away. He hid his face with an arm and didn't twitch a muscle. The spotlight probed the bush where he hid but moved on, the warrior staying stock-still until the vehicle disappeared around a corner of the house.

He resumed his slow crawl until he lay outside the band of light that edged the house. Another step and he would be within the scope of the floodlights and would be clearly visible to anyone who happened to glance in his direction.

He had to take the risk.

Bolan had chosen to enter through the front door. Smashing a side window was out of the question, and the rear door was at the end of a long expanse of patio near the swimming pool. While he fiddled with the back door, which might be bolted as well as locked, the warrior would be totally without cover for long seconds.

The front door was flanked by a pair of sculpted trees that reduced the visibility of anyone watching the front. Bolan was confident that he could pick the lock, so the door wouldn't be a barrier.

He took a last look around and dashed for the door. When he reached his objective he cursed under his breath. Tucked into the wall beside the door was an electronic key pad, a red light glowing below the numbers.

He should have expected an electronic alarm system. Unfortunately, there wasn't a lot he could do about it without some very sophisticated equipment that he didn't have with him at the moment.

His primary plan was blown to shreds. Bolan stepped into the shadow of a tree to consider his next move. He could, perhaps, still demolish the house by planting the explosives on the exterior. It might not be quite as effective, but he could deliver a powerful punch with the load of high explosives he had brought with him. There was a crawl space under the house, but that would be a last resort, as it was a place that more than likely would be searched before the VIPs arrived.

The engine of the patrol Jeep rumbled, and Bolan pressed himself deeper into the shadow of the tree. The vehicle screeched to a halt ten yards away, and two men climbed out.

Bolan drew an eight-inch combat knife and fingered off the safety of the silenced Beretta. If he was detected, he would try to deal with the guards without attracting the perimeter sentries. Then he'd have to scramble.

The Colombians sauntered up the walk, submachine guns slung carelessly over their shoulders. Bolan gleaned from their conversation that they were stopping for coffee. One remarked that what Cordero didn't know wouldn't hurt him, so the warrior guessed that this break wouldn't meet the approval of the Colombian commander.

Bolan watched with interest as one man punched a combination on the door pad, clearly visible from where the warrior stood rooted in the shadows. When the red alarm light winked off, the Colombians unlocked the door and stepped through.

He waited for a moment to see if the alarm light came on again. It stayed dark, so the big man moved from cover and opened the door a crack. He heard voices coming from somewhere deeper inside the house.

He slipped in and closed the door gently behind him. A light reflected to the left, probably from the kitchen. Bolan headed right and waited in the shadows of a darkened living room until the sounds of muted conversation ended and the front door opened and closed. He stayed in the living room until the Jeep pulled away.

Bolan began to search the sprawling house to determine the actual meeting room and the best place to deposit his surprise package.

A large study overlooking the pool had been converted into a conference room. A long table lined with a dozen chairs stood in the middle of the room, while straight-backed chairs for some of the assistants stood along the walls.

There were few places to conceal a bomb. The walls were solid, and he wouldn't risk the possibility of discovery by sticking it to the bottom of the table.

He stood on the table and raised one of the acoustic tiles that formed the ceiling. There was plenty of room for the explosives and timer, and it was unlikely that Cordero's henchmen would check up here.

He went to work, sticking the plastique to the metal supports that held the tiles. He implanted the remote-control detonator after verifying that it and the signal transmitter both functioned properly. As an afterthought he implanted a timer that would set off the bomb at four o'clock, two hours after the meeting was to begin, in case for some reason he was out of range of the transmitter.

After polishing the scuff marks off the table, Bolan returned to the front hall. The red alarm light glowed once more under the inside control pad. He punched in the code he had observed and the alarm switched off. He glanced through a glass panel in the door to check for sentries. Satisfied that the way was clear, he slipped out, pausing to relock the front door and to reengage the alarm system.

Bolan vanished into the night, confident that no one would ever know that he had come and gone—until the house vanished in a pillar of flame.

PINOLLA BUTTONHOLED BOLAN the next morning. "Any success last night?" he asked quietly.

"I think I know now exactly how I'll get in and out. There's a crawl space under the house where I can plant the bomb, but I'd like to know where the meeting room is."

"You don't have to shout, for Christ's sake," Pinolla complained. "Anyway, good work. I'll talk to you after the meeting and give you some more specifics of the inside of the house."

Bolan watched Pinolla leave. With any luck, Pinolla would be dead in a few hours. It gave the warrior a slight pause as he reflected on the nature of his life's endeavors. He knew well that Pinolla was the kingpin of a criminal empire that fed off human suffering, took advantage of people's weaknesses. The Fatman wouldn't hesitate to kidnap, intimidate, steal or murder if it served the interests of the Family. Intellectually Bolan knew that Pinolla and the others of his kind had to be put out of business. Permanently.

Pinolla had been convicted of crimes against humanity, and he had been judged and condemned in Bolan's mind.

Now it was time to fulfill his duty as Executioner.

BOLAN SAT in his quarters, which were much improved from those assigned to him at first, performing the daily maintenance to his weapons, ensuring that each was in perfect condition.

He glanced at his watch and noted that it was almost time to move out. The Mafia dons were going to gather at Pinolla's prior to traveling to the meeting site. Bolan intended to be long gone before they arrived.

Knuckles rapped on his door a microsecond before it was opened.

"You had better come to the house," Garibaldi growled. "There's trouble."

He refused to give any further information, so Bolan followed him to Pinolla's office. Inside, the don waited with two hardmen.

A young black woman in a maid's uniform was handcuffed to a chair. A trickle of blood had crept from her mouth and nose, dripping onto her starched white apron. One of her eyes was nearly puffed shut, and her lip was split.

"Meet Agent Angela Foster of the FBI," Pinolla announced, his eyes cold and hard. "Franco had discovered a couple of bugs in the place over the past couple of days. Then he started looking for how they were getting in here."

"Yeah," Garibaldi chimed in, gloating as he spoke. "While you were out playing Superman, I was here watching the boss's back. I caught her with a bug in her pocket." The lieutenant looked triumphant, as though he had settled a score with Bolan.

"You had better let me go," Foster said with some difficulty. "If I don't report in soon, the place will be swarming with Federal agents."

The office door swung open, and two enforcers dropped an older man on the floor. His hands were tied behind his back, and a spot of red showed through thin brown hair. He appeared to be unconscious.

"Randy!" Foster gasped.

One of the enforcers handed something across to Pinolla. "Special Agent Randolph W. Rawlins," the Fatman read. "Well, my dear, it looks as though we have your backup with us. And you, Foster, are on a high wire without a net. Be careful how the wind blows.''

"I think we should let them go," Bolan said. "They've got nothing on us now except a couple of lousy assault charges. That's nothing to a good lawyer. But if anything else happens to them, all that's going to change. The Feds and the cops will come down on us real hard.''

Pinolla looked at him, his eyes small and angry. "You don't know it, but I own everyone from the police commissioner to the mayor. Half the judges in this city are in my pocket. Something went wrong this time, but I should have known in advance that someone had infiltrated the staff. If anything happens to this pair, two gets you ten it'll never come to trial. If we go to court there won't be enough evidence to convict—you're going to make sure of it.''

Bolan tried again. "It might not be a good idea.''

Pinolla wouldn't listen to any objections. "That's not the way we do things in this organization. I'm going to keep the cops and the Feds off my back by showing a few people that Joey Pinolla still has what it takes. Now you've got two choices—prove your loyalty by taking care of this pair, or get the hell out now. What's it going to be?''

Bolan shrugged. If he didn't do something the Feds would be killed by someone else. The only way to save them was to give in.

"I'll take care of it.''

"Good. Tomaso there will go with you to help out with the heavy work. Wrap them up, Franco.''

The mobster placed tape over the agents' mouths and roped their hands and feet.

Bolan returned to his quarters for his weapons. By the time he got outside, the bound agents had been loaded into the back of a sedan and covered with a blanket.

"Are you set for the meet?" Bolan asked Pinolla, before he climbed into the car.

"I know the drill. Arrive fifteen minutes late to prepare for the next day. Franco will be with me and together we should be able to tell you everything you need to know. We'll see you back here later."

"Right."

As Bolan drove outside the city limits Tomaso began to protest. "I don't like it. Where the hell do you think you're going? We always either dump the stiffs in the ocean or plop them into quicksand in the Everglades. I don't think it's safe just to bury them in the woods somewhere."

"You don't have to think Tomaso. I'm in charge, so shut up." Bolan didn't much like the young, swaggering Mafia enforcer and didn't bother to hide it.

After about twenty minutes Bolan spotted a rural route and ordered Tomaso to take it. Two miles later they turned onto a dirt track and proceeded deep into the woods.

The hardman stopped the car at Bolan's command, and they got out. They hauled the agents from the car and laid them on the grass. The warrior noted that the injured man was awake and nervous. He obviously knew what was planned.

Bolan and his companion removed shovels from the trunk and began to dig in the hard soil.

"I got an idea," Tomaso suggested. "Let's not bother to whack them. Let's just bury them alive, starting at the feet, and leave them to choke. Great idea, huh?"

"You're a sick man. Shut up and dig."

"You're a real sweet guy. Don't you know how to have fun?"

Bolan didn't answer and the men dug in silence. After a minute the warrior threw down his shovel, drew the Beretta and leveled it at his companion.

Tomaso looked at him with astonishment. "What the hell are you doing?" Then he lifted his shovel and ran at Bolan, slashing with the curved blade at Bolan's neck.

The Executioner fired, and the howling lead bit into the man's heart, stopping his charge as though he'd run into a brick wall. The hardman toppled to the grass and rolled into the partly dug grave.

Bolan walked over the the prostrate agents. "Listen carefully. It doesn't matter who I am except that I'm associated with a federal organization that has been working Pinolla for a while. I can cover for you, but you both have to lay low for the next few days. You'll know when it's safe to come out." He removed the tape from their mouths. "Okay?"

They both agreed, grateful to be alive.

Bolan changed his mind about burying Tomaso and loaded his body into the trunk. He drove north with the two agents, evading all their attempts to pry information out of him. He left them with the vague impression that he was CIA. Finally they reached their destination, a vacation condo that Randy owned near Hillsboro Beach.

Bolan glanced at his watch. It was a quarter to four, which meant that in minutes the meeting should be coming to an explosive end.

PINOLLA WAS RESTLESS. The meeting had been going on for an hour, and no progress whatsoever had been made. The mafioso didn't particularly care what happened in the sessions. He was simply anxious to get the day over with and get on to the real business of wiping out the Colombians.

The room held four of the cartel chiefs and six Mafia dons. It had been decided earlier that the guards from both sides would remain outside the room, where they would watch one another warily, weapons at the ready.

Down the table, Zambioni from Chicago was droning on, raising difficulties and listing objections. Pinolla tried to look interested. The only point of the discussion today was to lull the Colombians into believing that the Mafia was truly sincere in wanting to resolve their differences.

Pinolla watched the Colombians. In addition to Cordero there were three more major players from the central committee in Medellín. Something about them didn't ring true. Although there was nothing obvious, the one called Rico, in particular, looked as though he were grinning inside, laughing at some secret joke he wasn't about to share.

The Fatman had studied human nature his entire life, and he knew that he was pretty good at reading below the surface. Although Cordero had a poker face as good as any, the occasional surreptitious glances he shot at Pinolla were filled with malice.

Pinolla glanced at his watch. It was only five minutes before four o'clock, and it had been agreed that the meeting would run until six. Don Zambioni finally ended his speech, and the Fatman jumped in before anyone else could speak to propose a short break. The suggestion was readily accepted.

Most of the chiefs headed for a table of canapés and drinks. Pinolla noticed that Cordero made for the interior of the house.

The Fatman pushed through sliding doors that led to the patio. He walked over to the pool, more inclined for fresh air than booze and doubletalk in a small, smoky room.

He stood by the pool, thinking that the water looked inviting and refreshing. The only time his feet didn't hurt was when he was swimming. He could roll over on his back and float for hours. It was the only advantage of being fat.

A thunderous wave of sound crashed over him, pounding on his eardrums like a jackhammer. A fraction of a second later an invisible hand shoved him hard in the back, and the Fatman toppled facefirst into the pool.

He came up sputtering and coughing. Pinolla held his nose and ducked down in a hurry as burning chunks of wood splashed hissing in the water around his head. He squatted under water and held his breath until his lungs felt like liquid fire. When he finally came gasping to the surface, the rain of fiery debris had ended.

The house was a shambles, totally demolished. Wood, masonry and furniture had been smashed into fist-size chunks. Fires burned among the devastated wreckage, and a slight breeze carried the revolting stench of burned flesh to his nostrils.

Broken bodies lay all around, tossed and torn by the power of the blast. The guards who had stood outside the patio door lay scattered like leaves blown by the wind.

Pinolla climbed the steps out of the pool and ran, water flying from him as if he were a wet dog shaking itself. The compound resembled a battlefield, the dead sprawled in unnatural positions, the wounded crying for assistance.

The Fatman ignored them all. Rescue teams would be there soon enough to aid the injured. In the meantime he wanted nothing more than to get as far away as possible.

He reached his limousine, which had been dented by falling bits of the house but was otherwise undamaged. His chauffeur was ready to go. The confused drivers of the other dons called to him for an explanation, but he brushed them aside.

He climbed in back and ordered the driver through the now-deserted front gate. Everyone inside must have died, he realized. A lot of the Families would be looking for new chieftains.

Pinolla poured himself a tall bourbon from the compact back-seat bar and tossed it down, his shaking hand spilling most of it over his shirtfront. Another followed it down his throat moments later.

The Fatman sloshed a third drink into his glass and began to think. With the whole eastern U.S. Mafia crippled, there must be a way for him to gain a little something out of the disaster, provided he could absolve himself of any responsibility. Obviously it had to have been Cordero's fault entirely, in spite of the fact that the Colombian gangster had to be dead.

At least that was one positive result: he was alive and Cordero was human confetti.

13

Bolan turned the ignition key and shifted the car into gear. Some unfortunate driver had wiped out in spectacular fashion a few hundred yards ahead, and the big man had been stuck in traffic while the police sorted out the mess.

It was well after five o'clock. The plastique had already blown, and there was no point in driving by the meeting place.

Bolan drove back to the Pinolla mansion, intending to stay just long enough to search for something that might be added to Brognola's growing file on the Family. He wasn't prepared to see Pinolla's limousine when his own vehicle turned into the long drive that led to the mansion.

The Fatman stepped out of the limo as Bolan drew abreast of it. "Where the hell have you been?" Pinolla demanded when Bolan got out of the car.

"There was some trouble."

"You think you got trouble!" Pinolla said. He started to laugh, great bellows and guffaws that continued so long that it seemed as if he had lost his grip on reality. The mobster gained control of himself with an effort. "Come inside," he ordered.

When they were seated in the study, Pinolla began to talk. He rambled for half an hour, relating the full story of the explosion in graphic detail.

Bolan was relieved to hear that his plan had basically succeeded. Casualties had evidently been heavy. "Any survivors?" he asked.

Pinolla sipped at his bourbon. "I called the hospital and checked up. Glisenti, Moscetto and Zambioni are dead for sure. The guys from Philly and New York are in critical condition and not expected to make it. A few of my men made it back here unharmed or just a little banged up, but a lot of them are dead or badly injured, including Franco."

"What about the Colombians?"

"All the leaders are dead, I think. Nobody could have survived the blast in the house."

"What do you think happened?"

Pinolla took a long swallow of bourbon. "I think that snake Cordero planned to whack us the same way we were going to get him. He screwed up somehow and triggered the bomb early."

Bolan didn't disagree. If that was what Pinolla believed, he'd go along with it. "What do you plan to do now?"

"I believe it's time someone took charge of the situation before it gets out of hand. Those Colombians are all maniacs, wackos. Let's keep them offshore and let business here be run by real Americans."

"So does that mean you're going to try to kick the Colombians out completely?"

Pinolla smiled slyly. "We'll see about that. Cocaine is too valuable to abandon, but if we can keep those South American lizards out of the U.S. it will be better for the rest of us. Maybe those other guys getting knocked off wasn't such a bad thing for Joey Pinolla. I think that I can guide the new leaders of those Families. Together we can declare a vendetta on the Colombians and erase them from this part of the country.''

Bolan smiled at the mafioso's boldness. Always calculating, he saw an opportunity to bring the Families under his ironhanded control. "You'd be the godfather to them all.''

Pinolla spread his hands modestly. ''I might be the best man alive for the job. Now tell me, are those snoopers out of the way?''

Bolan related how he'd been busy trying to bury the male cop when Tomaso decided to have some fun with the woman. She got hold of his gun and shot him dead. Bolan then shot the girl, disposed of the bodies and brought Tomaso back in the trunk.

Pinolla didn't seem very concerned. ''Tomaso was always a wild kid, especially where women were involved. I'm not surprised he ended this way. Dump his body somewhere it will be found, and we'll tell his mama that the Colombians got him. Come back here and we'll plan how to take care of the rest of the Colombians in the area while they're still reeling and leaderless.''

The phone on Pinolla's desk rang, and he picked it up.

''Fatman,'' the voice said, quavering with anger, ''this is Jaime Cordero. I'm going to get you for what you did.''

The line went dead.

CORDERO REPLACED the phone in the cradle gingerly. His arm hurt. So did his back, along with every other muscle in his body. But he wasn't complaining. At the time of the explosion, he'd been in the washroom, and the one-piece steel bathtub and shower had fallen on him like a jar placed over a frog. In spite of bruising him badly, it had protected him from the debris until a rescue team dug him out an hour later.

Cordero had been lucky. He couldn't say the same for Rico or the other two visitors from the central committee of the cartel. There hadn't been enough left of the three of them to fill a decent-size garbage bag.

The last laugh was on Rico. The little man had insisted on handling security himself and had convinced the other two VIPs to come up on his say-so. Now that the little viper was dead, Cordero had been able to pin the blame on him.

Rico was in no position to contradict him.

Cordero's hand had been reinforced for the short term. Now his only task was revenge and the elimination of Pinolla's organization. Someone had obviously gotten through to plant the bomb that ravaged the conference room and obliterated many of Cordero's men. He suspected it was the same man who had dogged him and frustrated his plans at nearly every turn since he had appeared in Pinolla's camp.

What the Colombian couldn't understand was why the bomb had been detonated while the Mafia men were still at the meeting. It looked like Pinolla's mercenary had finally made a serious mistake.

Cordero felt more confident than ever. He had survived the worst that Pinolla could throw at him. Now it was time for some pitching of his own.

BOLAN QUIETLY UNLOCKED the rear door of the Pinolla mansion. It was three in the morning, a time when the warrior knew he'd encounter little opposition on his way to the study where he hoped to find the safe that held the Fatman's secret files.

The big man had already evaded several of Pinolla's sentries as they patrolled the perimeter of the estate. Twice as many men as usual had been assigned guard duty since the Mafia don had taken Cordero's threat seriously. The Fatman was prepared for an assault.

Bolan was dressed in civilian clothes but carried a black knapsack filled with safe-cracking equipment. If he was discovered and pressed for an explanation of why he was in the house he could plausibly maintain that he had come to test the evening guards.

Bolan catfooted through the silent house and paused at the door to the study. His pick flashed and the door swung open. Before he stood to enter the room a floorboard creaked behind him.

"Don't move another inch."

Bolan turned slowly, silently cursing himself. He'd been so absorbed in picking the lock that someone had gotten the drop on him.

A big bruiser had him covered with a pistol identical to the Executioner's Beretta 93-R. The big man recognized the guy, but didn't know his name. Bolan decided to try to bluff it out.

"You know who I am, don't you?" Bolan asked.

The hit man nodded reluctantly.

"I'm here to test the inside security. Now that you've found me, just tell me your name and I'll go back to bed. I'll make sure that you get a gold star tomorrow."

The guard hesitated, then lowered his gun.

Bolan struck with lightning speed, dropping his hand to his belt and pulling free a flat throwing knife. With one motion he threw it underhand with all the force he could muster.

It flew straight and true, stabbing into the guy's throat. He slid to the floor, his hands clutching spasmatically at the haft of the knife.

The warrior grabbed the dead man by his feet and dragged him into the study. He deposited the corpse behind Pinolla's massive cherry desk. The irony of the cadaver at Pinolla's feet brought a grim smile to Bolan's lips.

He began a rapid professional search of the room, pulling books from the shelves and dumping drawers on the floor. In a few minutes the room was a wreck, but Bolan was no farther ahead. After convincing himself that the safe was somewhere else, he splintered the lock to the gun room beyond the office.

He snapped off the study light and walked into the gun museum. He resumed his search, tugging methodically at the gun cases that lined the walls, looking for a hidden catch.

Bolan stopped dead in his tracks when he detected the rattle of a key in the study door. He raced to the door, drawing his silenced Beretta as he moved.

The study door popped open and a hardman named Mario stepped into the room, his hand gripping his pistol. He stopped with a gasp as he flicked on the light and surveyed the trashed inner sanctum.

The Executioner squeezed off a shot and the 9 mm slug pulverized Mario's teeth before it chopped through the medulla. The brain shut down in a split second, and the gunner collapsed.

Bolan tugged Mario through the door and placed him beside his companion.

He resumed the search, ears cocked for further interruptions. A few minutes later he grabbed the butt of a Heckler & Koch G-11 Caseless Rifle. He was rewarded as the entire case unlatched and popped out an inch. Bolan tugged gently and the case folded back quietly to expose a safe that would have been appropriate for a bank.

Bolan pulled an electronic sensor from his pack and placed it over the tumblers. He spun the dial slowly until a red light glowed, indicating that he had triggered the first number. He repeated the procedure three more times until the bolt unlatched with a soft click.

The big man examined the interior of the safe with interest. Cocaine lay on shelves in plastic bags beside a black bag filled with Krugerrands; crisp hundred-dollar bills were lined up in neat stacks; a jewel box held a fortune in rings and necklaces.

Obviously crime did pay in Pinolla's case.

At least until he had run across the Executioner.

Bolan turned to record boxes that occupied the bulk of the safe. A cursory examination showed that most of the paper was of little value in the larger scheme of things. However, there were a few gems such as the record of bribes and hush money lavished on officials under Pinolla's control. The warrior recognized several names, including one high-ranking man in the Justice Department. Another volume contained correspondence that nailed down the entire drug distribution network along the East Coast.

He dropped the most vital pieces of information into his pack. They would make for fascinating reading in Brognola's hands. Bolan added the kilos of cocaine, intending to dispose of the white powder at the first opportunity. He left the safe open and printed a short note that he left on the jewel case.

As the Executioner was about to leave he heard a voice in the corridor outside the study calling for Mario. He hugged the wall beside the door and drew a garrote.

The door opened and a head poked in. "Mario, are you in there?" the watchman asked.

Bolan snaked the thin metal band over the intruder's head and jerked on the handles. The wire bit into the hardman's throat, choking off his wind. The sentry struggled wildly, but the warrior applied more pressure and the man's movements gradually subsided. Bolan released his hold and the corpse crumpled to the floor.

Bolan picked up his knapsack and returned to his quarters. Along the way he stashed his pack in a storage shed under a rusting wheelbarrow.

Half an hour later pandemonium broke out as someone ran through the barracks, yelling for everyone to wake up. Bolan rushed out with his Desert Eagle in hand, half-dressed and looking as if he'd just been awakened.

Mafia hardmen had gathered in Pinolla's study and out in the corridor beyond. Bolan elbowed his way through the crowd into the room. An angry murmur ran through the gunmen at the sight of the bodies.

Pinolla stood by the door to his gun room, wearing a striped bathrobe that made him look as though he were encased in a small circus tent. He was pale, but his eyes blazed with anger.

"Now listen up," he said. The buzzing of the crowd subsided. "You've seen the bodies. Are we going to stand for this?"

The group of men replied with a resounding "no."

"All right. Our caller left a message. Here it is. 'I could have cut your throat and left you here with your useless henchmen,'" he read, "'but the time has not yet come for me to kill you. You have much more to suffer. I have left your gold and jewels. I would not want your widow to starve. Cordero.'"

The crowd buzzed at the message until the Fatman called for silence.

"I'm sure that you're all as enraged as I am," he said. "Cordero has injured the organization in a way that can never be forgiven. I declare the vendetta against him and all his men. I will not rest until that Colombian bastard is buried."

The gunmen broke into wild applause. Pinolla ordered a few men to dispose of the bodies and clean the room, and told Bolan and another man to follow him.

The three men sat in the living room near a beautifully crafted statue of the Virgin Mary. "Pietro," Pinolla began, "you're my head of security. Explain yourself."

Pietro stammered through an apology, telling Pinolla that although numerous guards were posted, none of them had detected even the smallest sign of the Colombians.

"You've failed me, Pietro, and I can no longer trust you in your post. Go." The mafioso crept away, angered and embarrassed by his dismissal.

"You're the only man I can trust," Pinolla said to Bolan.

"Don't worry, Don Pinolla. I'll take care of you."

14

Jaime Cordero stood before the street toughs, his face a frozen mask. He concealed his rage behind an icy facade and addressed the three gang leaders he'd invited to his home. "I called you here today because I wanted privacy to discuss a matter that could be very important to your gangs—and very lucrative."

"Don't jive us, man," Curtis Augustine said. "The word on the street is that the Fatman has wasted most of your dudes. I figure you called us here because you need us to make sure he don't waste you, too."

Cordero chose his words carefully before replying. It was clear that more was known about his situation than he would have liked, and the gang leaders realized that they dealt from a position of strength. It was for them an enjoyable reversal of their usual role. Cordero ordinarily patronized them as low-class scum, and the gangs depended on the Colombians for their supplies of dope.

Cordero despised the gangs and wouldn't have asked to meet with them unless driven by an urgent need. And everyone in the room knew it.

Curtis Augustine represented the Bloods. Above the red scarf that represented the gang colors he sported a white felt hat and Ferrari shades. His gold chains hung in a solid three-inch band, and a diamond-clustered Cartier watch glittered on his wrist.

The largest of the Hispanic gangs was led by Manuel Mendez. Although the young man appeared serious and rather shy, Cordero's sources told him that Manuel had become leader of Los Bravos as much by his skill with a knife as by his personal magnetism. The ebony-handled knife he had left with Cordero's bodyguards had twenty-one notches in the haft.

The last gang leader was known simply as Jimmy, warlord of the local Jamaicans. Stringy dreadlocks hung from below his knitted cap onto the shoulders of the orange-and-yellow caftan that loosely draped his body. Round granny glasses perched on the edge of his nose. Although he looked like a refugee from a hostel, his hobby was collecting antique Rolls-Royces.

Jimmy and his compatriots were the wild card. Ferocious and fond of automatic weapons, they were often too stoned to be totally reliable. Usually the Jamaicans were kept at a safe distance, but Cordero thought that he could control them, like any lethal weapon, long enough to aim them at Pinolla.

His greatest problem would be to keep the gangs from one another's throats long enough to reach a viable agreement.

"It is true," Cordero said, "that I have suffered some setbacks in the war between Pinolla and myself, although the extent of those losses has been greatly exaggerated. Pinolla is in far worse shape than I am."

"That's not what I heard," Curtis interrupted.

"Look, if you prefer to deal with Pinolla, then get the hell out!" Cordero let a little of his anger show for effect. "If you want to listen to what I propose, shut up!" The Colombian glared at the Blood leader, daring him to leave.

Curtis had been called. Was he in or out?

"Be cool, dude," Curtis soothed. He had no intention of letting the other two remain behind and maybe cut him out of a lucrative deal. "If we're going to rap, get on with it. Just don't jive us, hey?"

Cordero stared down the Hispanic and the Jamaican in turn until they refused to meet his eyes. The Colombian smiled grimly and felt a certain amount of relief.

The cartel had given him a last chance to redeem himself, provided he could do it without any more assistance. However, their patience had just about run out. The Colombian needed the gangs even more than they suspected. Now that his bluff had worked and he had established that he was still in charge, the criminal clique could get down to business.

There was a war to be fought, but the killing couldn't start until his allies were bought and paid for.

PINOLLA SMELLED a very large, hungry rat.

A contrite Cordero had just called, proposing an alliance between the warring parties, with the Mafia as senior partner. If you can't beat them, join them, the Colombian had claimed with apparent sincerity.

The Mafia don had simply listened, promising nothing except that he would get back to him with an answer. Pinolla knew that it was a trap. His only problem was tactical. Would there be more advantage in smashing the Colombians in an arranged confrontation, or should he launch a secret strike at his own choosing?

The Fatman sought out his security chief, finding the big man in an outbuilding that housed a firing range.

Pinolla walked beside Bolan as the taller man strolled down a line of shooters without comment, examining the paper targets they shot at. The Mafia don found it a very depressing experience. His men were lousy shots.

"What did you want to see me about?" Bolan asked.

Pinolla relayed the contents of the peculiar phone call from Cordero and added his own suspicions.

"There isn't a clear answer," the big man replied. "If you refuse outright, Cordero will know he has nothing left to lose and will come gunning for you. If you go after him first he might anticipate your move and be waiting for you. If he's well prepared, he could massacre your men."

"What if I agree to meet in a few days and hit him in the meantime?"

"The same thing applies. He might be anticipating precisely that and plan to smash you in the interim. No. I think you should meet as soon as possible, tonight if he'll agree. That way he has less time to prepare or to do something radical like take you out with a sniper shot."

Pinolla turned a little pale, not having considered that possibility. The Fatman hastily moved Bolan into the main house.

"What if I'm just playing into his hands by agreeing to meet? He'll probably plan not to show up and to ambush me when I arrive."

"Leave things to me," Bolan said. "That's exactly what I expect, except that we'll get there first. You can stay here, and I'll report back when we've eliminated his enforcers."

"You're gambling with the lives of my soldiers," Pinolla complained.

Bolan shrugged. "Okay. If you prefer to remain locked in your study for the rest of your life, that's up to you. That is, if you'll be safe even there."

"I thought you claimed you could handle the security job for me," Pinolla said, thinking of the bodies piled grotesquely behind his desk.

"If my advice isn't of any value to you, it's time for me to move on."

The two men locked eyes. Pinolla read a determination that sent chills down his spine.

"All right," the Fatman sighed, "you're the military expert. I'll do as you suggest."

"Then set it up for tonight if you can," Bolan said, writing some notes on a piece of paper. "Set it up for any one of these sites. Now if you'll excuse me, I have work to do."

BOLAN JOGGED across the treeline, checking the positions of his men. A dozen Mafia soldiers had been hard at work for the past several hours, preparing foxholes and shelters.

As the daylight faded, the warrior stalked around the small open meadow that would shortly be transformed into a killing ground. He stood in the center of the clearing, satisfied with the handiwork of the men. He could see each of the hidden mafia soldiers, but only because he knew exactly where to look. Enshrouded by a cloak of darkness, the gunners would be completely invisible. Even if they were pinpointed by the muzzle-flashes of their weapons, they would be far better protected than their assailants.

The Executioner, however, would know precisely where to find the Mafia killers.

He called the troops over and gave them their final orders. Everyone was to return to his place and wait for the fight to start. No one was to fire until Bolan started the shooting for their side.

The signal would be obvious.

Bolan knew that show time would begin not long after dark. He was certain that Cordero would move in force and had proposed this rendezvous as a final gambit to crush the Mafia forces. The warrior anticipated a shoot-out and had disposed his force to catch most of the Colombian's attack team in a withering cross fire.

He sent away the cars that had provided transport, keeping only three long limousines that had been parked in the center of the woodland.

The warrior moved silently through the trees on his inspection, leaving his weapon cached under a fallen tree trunk. Pinolla's men were equipped with Ingram MAC-10s, adequate short-range weapons in the hands of unskilled marksmen.

Bolan had borrowed an M-16A2 assault rifle from the Fatman's collection. The weapon was an improved version of the prior model, incorporating a 3-shot mode in addition to the single shot and automatic modes. A new flash suppressor and compensator reduced muzzle-flash and dust dispersion.

Bolan had taken a short trip off the estate to buy ammunition for the rifle. The excursion also provided an opportunity for him to retrieve the sack of documents he had stashed the night before. The warrior had delivered the papers to a drop spot where they would be collected and delivered to Hal Brognola. He had also dumped several kilos of cocaine down a sewer.

As darkness turned into night the evening came alive with nocturnal sounds. Bats whirled in the sky, feeding on the tiny night fliers. Toads croaked, and the occasional rustle in the underground marked the passage of a larger animal.

Bolan retrieved the assault rifle, settled into a flanking position and waited. His ears filtered out the normal sounds of dusk as he listened for the unusual. A pair of night-vision goggles gave him a futuristic, alien appearance. Night descended completely, and the sliver of moon became obscured by thin, drifting clouds. The beams of Pinolla's limousines stabbed through the blackness, illuminating hundreds of tiny bugs dancing in the light.

The animal and insect noises couldn't fully cover the sounds of men approaching through the woods. Bolan heard a swiftly choked-off curse before he saw the first of the enemy three hundred yards from his position.

At first only a couple of scouts probed the clearing, flitting from tree to tree. Bolan froze as they passed, hoping that his ambush wouldn't be discovered.

Apparently his men's camouflage passed muster, as a wave from the patrol leader brought a small flood of men pouring into the woods.

As far as Bolan could tell, the attackers numbered about fifty, obviously unskilled and uncomfortable in the dark. Their arrival was heralded by a crescendo of cracking twigs and slapping branches. There were a few loud grunts as some of them tripped over tree roots.

In a few minutes the woods returned to a nearly normal level of silence as the invaders settled uneasily into firing positions around the clearing.

The gunners were a mixed bag of blacks and Hispanics, dressed in a wild assortment of combat garb that ranged from slogan-emblazoned T-shirts to shiny leather pants. Their weapons ran the gamut from a few Saturday-night specials to military-issue M-16s.

Some of the ambushers were nearly on top of the well-hidden foxholes of the Mafiosi. It was almost beyond belief that they hadn't noticed the dug-in defenders.

Then the waiting game began again.

It had been agreed that each side would bring only three cars. To prevent treachery no one was supposed to get out of the vehicles until Cordero flashed the lights of his car. Then the bodyguards would climb from their cars to search the area and establish a secure perimeter. Only then would Cordero and Pinolla climb into the ring to spar.

Pinolla's vehicles were already in place, and occupied the far side of the clearing. To all indications the Mafia chief was keeping his part of the bargain to the letter.

Lights shone in the distance, waving and bouncing as a short line of cars negotiated the rough track that wound through the forest. Three stretch limousines pulled into the far side of the clearing, with Cordero's flashy white Mercedes bringing up the rear. The procession ground to a halt with the first two vehicles drawing abreast and Cordero's personal car in the background, bathing Pinolla's cars in their beams. The lead limo flashed its lights once, twice.

The Colombian allies opened fire, flame belching from fifty weapons. A storm of lead crashed into Pinolla's fleet, sweeping them from bumper to bumper. Glass in the car windows disappeared, hammered into fragments under the savage assault. The clearing reverberated with the sounds of blazing gunfire.

The firing trailed off slowly as the attackers gradually exhausted their ammunition until the last gunner lowered his weapon.

Only a few buzzing insects disturbed the sudden silence. Nothing moved among the blasted wreckage of Pinolla's miniconvoy.

A whoop from the ambushers shattered the stillness. Self-congratulaton rang from one group to another as they celebrated the destruction of the enemy force.

A dozen Colombians poured from the two crew wagons and advanced toward the bullet-holed vehicles. Headlights illuminated an array of small arms that were pointed at the wreckage by the advancing Colombian hit men, vigilant in case anyone had miraculously survived.

In moments the Colombians and their allies would be close enough to the Mafia limos to detect that they had been deceived. Bolan sighted his M-16 on the wary Colombian who led the probe.

The Executioner opened fire.

The M-16 vibrated in his grasp as he blazed away on full-auto. The Colombians whirled and staggered in the harsh glare of their headlights as Bolan waved the assault rifle back and forth. Blood sprayed from wounds like a fine mist, coating the polished black metal of the limos and the grass meadow.

A few of the quicker hit men dived for the cover of Pinolla's battered cars.

A moment after Bolan triggered his initial burst, the hidden Mafia gunners joined in. The massed submachine gun fire scythed through the ranks of the enemy, turning victory into panic.

Cordero's men went to ground quickly. Some of them tumbled in bloody heaps as the Mafia fire bored into their vitals, while others were able to crawl for the relative safety of the tree line. A few returned fire—those who hadn't spent their stock of ammunition in a reckless blaze of fireworks aimed at the empty cars.

Bolan ejected an empty clip and loaded another, changing positions as he did. The sounds of running feet and slapping tree branches told the warrior that many of the men who had hung back in the woods instead of coming forward were making their escape, fleeing for their lives without a moment's consideration for their comrades in the clearing.

A wise if cowardly move, Bolan judged.

Cordero's limousine had pulled back almost the instant the first shot had been fired. The Colombian drug lord was probably halfway to Miami by now, busy with the important job of looking after number one.

Bolan had only a moment to regret that the Colombian had escaped. He had planned the ambush to catch the maximum number of gunmen in his sights, not sure that Cordero would even show for the meet.

The Executioner was willing to postpone payback time. Cordero only had a few hours to live.

The warrior began the task of picking a target, firing and changing position. He did this repeatedly with the skill of the marksman that he was. Bolan had to move frequently because he was in as much danger from the Mafia gunners as from the Colombians. Every shot he took brought rounds from the Mafia trenches, homing on his firing position. Pinolla's troops had no way of knowing who was behind the gun sight they were aiming at. However, they also had no way of knowing Bolan was playing a double game and marking up a score on both sides.

Occasionally he switched targets to pick off a Mafia gunner lying out of sight in a foxhole. Bolan had no love for the Mafia hardmen, and this was a perfect opportunity to reduce Pinolla's band to a manageable size.

Within a short time, the Fatman's name would come up on his death list. Every man left alive now would stand against him later on.

The firing in the area had died down considerably as targets became scarce. Surviving members of the assault force were being very cautious.

A knot of resistance had formed in the clearing—half a dozen of the Colombians had climbed inside the Mafia limos, hoping that the wrecked vehicles would afford some protection from the withering storm of fire coming at them from two sides.

Bolan knew that he had them at his mercy. They wouldn't have carried much ammunition with them for what should have been a simple hit-and-git operation. They had already shot a lot of it and would be running short.

Rather than trying an assault on their position, Bolan was content to wait them out. He was confident that they would make their move soon.

The Colombians were in an impossible position, and they knew it. If they were going to escape they would have to run the gauntlet of fire back to their limos. Otherwise they would be slowly picked off one at a time when the Mafia force eventually closed in on them.

An easier way out would be to break for the nearest patch of wood and make their way through the forest to the road. Bolan doubted, however, that this strategy would occur to the Colombians. They were too used to the urban fighter's dependence on the automobile.

Bolan shot up another Mafia emplacement and tumbled into the brush at the edge of the clearing as return fire hummed over his head. He ran to his left and took up a position that allowed him to cover the open ground between the two groups of cars.

The cornered Colombians stormed into activity, loosing a sudden barrage of gunfire. The Executioner suspected that this was the prelude to an escape attempt. He held his fire. Seconds later one of the Colombians shot out the headlights of their cars—an intelligent maneuver, as they couldn't have moved an inch away from cover without being silhouetted against the beams of light.

With one last burst of covering fire the Colombians ran for their cars.

The Executioner wasn't bothered by the sudden darkness. His night goggles showed the runners clearly enough to line up the M-16 target.

He squeezed the trigger in quick bursts, letting the Colombians run into the death stream he laid down. He led the targets perfectly and the gunners tumbled like dominos, falling to the ground in untidy heaps.

The last man tripped over the bodies of his fellows and fell, twisting. His trigger finger shot a final burst into the sky, a futile gesture marking his death.

Bolan had won another battle.

Now it was time to finish the war.

15

Cordero had given the order for retreat as soon as gun-fire erupted around the perimeter of the clearing. His men had started to drop to the ground, dying, but the crime lord wasn't interested in sticking around to find out how the battle turned out. He'd come to gloat over a turkey shoot, not to enter into the middle of a war zone. The only reason he had put in an appearance in the first place was because his allies had insisted he join them at the shoot-out.

His one thought was to get the hell out of the firing zone. The soldiers could look after themselves. If they didn't make it there wasn't much he could do about that.

His companions weren't pleased with the decision.

Jimmy, Curtis and Mendez were passengers in the limousine. The gang leaders had insisted on being present at the kill, since they had supplied most of the men for the ambush. Now they were shouting at Cordero to go back and rescue their men.

"Are you fools?" Cordero yelled. "What do you think you can accomplish besides get us all killed? Four more men can't change anything. They will have to live or die on their own."

"They need leaders or they'll all be slaughtered," Curtis said. He sat directly across from Cordero and leaned forward, his face inches from the drug lord's.

"Besides, I'm no coward. I've never run from a fight before."

"It's not cowardice when there's nothing to be gained by staying," Cordero insisted. "You may not mind getting killed for nothing, but I do. We're not going back."

"You're mistaken," Curtis announced, pulling a compact Glock 17 pistol from a pocket and aiming it point-blank at Cordero. "We *are* going back. Order your driver to turn around, or I'll shoot you. Are you guys with me?" He half turned to his companions.

The two other gang leaders nodded.

Cordero looked from one to the other. There weren't a lot of choices. "All right," he said. "I'll call the driver."

The car swung around fast, throwing the passengers against the padded sides of the limo. Curtis was sandwiched between the other two gang bosses.

Cordero seized his opportunity and fired a small Heckler & Koch F-7 pistol right through the pocket of his leather jacket. The first round caught Curtis in the groin, while a second bullet severed his jugular and finished the job.

The Jamaican jumped for Cordero as the Colombian pulled the pistol from his pocket. Cordero squeezed off a shot with the pistol almost touching Jimmy's chin. The guy pitched facefirst onto Cordero in a foam of blood and brain, knocking the Colombian's F-7 to the folds of the back seat.

Mendez jumped into the fray when he saw the sudden opportunity. Cordero fought hand to hand with his life as the prize, while the car bumped along the rough road. Mendez scored with short jabs to Cordero's body, as his other hand sought to cripple the Colombian with punches to the groin.

Cordero knew how to fight dirty as well, a legacy of years on the Medellín streets. He fought an arm free and scratched at Mendez's cheek, his long fingernails drawing blood. The Hispanic leader grunted with pain, but only swung harder.

The Colombian reached higher and a probing finger caught Mendez's eye. The gang leader screamed, and Cordero saw his opening, shooting his right hand forward with the knuckles held rigidly in a karate jab. His long arm connected with Mendez's Adam's apple, shattering it. Blood flowed down the guy's windpipe and he started to choke to death.

Cordero sucked air into his thirsty lungs as Mendez gasped out his life in front of him. He called the driver on the car phone and the limo screeched to a halt. The Colombian flung the two corpses and Mendez out the door. Mendez struggled feebly to rise from the cold pavement, but his wiry limbs had lost their whipcord strength.

Cordero got out of the car and began to kick Mendez with his pointed alligator boots. The Colombian grunted with the savage effort and was rewarded with the occasional crack as ribs or other small bones broke under the punishment.

Finally, when his leg felt too sore and heavy to swing any more, Cordero stopped. Mendez lay sprawled like a toy tossed from a ten-story building.

Cordero spit on each of the bleeding corpses, climbed into the car and ordered the driver back to his base. He had many things to do and time was running short.

WHEN THERE WERE no further movements among the crumpled heaps scattered around the clearing, Bolan blew his whistle for the all clear.

The few survivors climbed from their foxholes. They displayed the shock and stupefaction that Bolan had sometimes seen on troops fresh from a particularly bloody firefight.

However, they were the victors. The proof lay torn and bleeding almost at their feet. The Colombian hit men and their allies had paid the price for Cordero's ambition.

There was one final act to perform in this particular drama. Unless Bolan was very wrong, Cordero had finally had enough. The only question in the warrior's mind was when and where the drug lord would flee.

Several Mafia cars had been stashed on the other side of the woods. Bolan ordered a pair of hardmen who were slightly wounded to drive back to Pinolla and give him the news.

The warrior and the remainder of the men climbed into a sedan and headed for Cordero's mansion. The big man glanced at his watch. They had mounted pursuit in good time, but he wondered if they'd been quick enough. If Bolan had been in the same difficult position as Cordero, he wouldn't have hung around a second longer than necessary.

Minutes later he arrived at the gangster's estate. Cordero's massive limousine squatted in the driveway. Lights gleamed in nearly every window, and guards visibly patrolled the grounds in pairs.

The warrior pulled the car to a halt a block away, instructing the Mafia gunners to snipe at the guards from the perimeter wall. Bolan was going over the top and directly into the house while the defenders were occupied by the diversion.

Once inside he'd hunt down the drug lord and put an end to his murderous scheming.

Bolan fixed a time with one of the gunners to begin the assault. The warrior would prowl around to the rear of the property and make his approach through a line of least resistance.

Bolan drove the car back the way he had come and halted beyond Cordero's property. The Mafia hardmen were moving up in his wake and would assault near the front gate, sucking the Colombian defenders forward.

The warrior left his car and paused to reload his combat webbing with spare clips for the M-16. He ran toward the water, flitting from tree to tree with the assault rifle in hand. The Beretta and Desert Eagle rode under his jacket.

As the warrior jogged the last few yards to the wall, the sounds of machine guns chattering erupted at his back. Bolan crouched at the junction of the wall and the high cliff overlooking the bay. The wall was made of dressed granite topped by sharp black spikes, and it stretched a foot above his head. Bolan slung the rifle and levered himself up. He took a quick look over the fence and was relieved to see that the area in front of his crossing point was deserted. He hoisted a knee onto the wall between the spikes and pulled himself up and over.

Bolan landed softly in a flower bed on the other side and pressed back into the shadows. He unslung his rifle and spent a moment assessing the situation.

Fifty feet away a staircase zigzagged down the cliff to the water and a small marina. To the right of the staircase was a pool and a raised veranda. French doors opened from the mansion onto the pool deck. Spotlights covered the exterior in an almost daylight glow. The house itself was two stories high and of a modern design like the curve of a firm breast, constructed of soft curves that bulged out in front. No matter where Bolan tried to enter he would be exposed momentarily as he passed through the glare of the beams.

A gun battle raged in front of the house. The Mafia gunners were clustered by the gate and sniped down the curving driveway. The Colombians fired from the front windows of the house, as well as from behind sculptures on the lawn.

The Mafia enforcers were badly outgunned by the Colombians, but that didn't matter as they had no intention of actually trying to break through the defenses. They served their purpose by acting as a decoy while Bolan made his end run.

The warrior examined the exposed ground in front of him once more and decided to make his way through one of the doors opening onto the pool.

Bolan gripped the M-16 and sprinted for the patio.

CORDERO JUMPED to his feet as the sound of gunfire rippled through the house. He crossed to the window and looked cautiously out at the grounds. Red flashes punctured the dark, and the drug lord noted with relief that there were far more gunners on his side than on the attackers'.

He resumed his hasty packing, confident that his men could hold off the assault force until he had completed his frantic preparations for flight. He'd already filled one tough gym bag with a mixture of documents and cold cash. He intended to take enough liquid capital to enable him to disappear for a very long time.

The gang leader had already decided that his destination would be somewhere foreign and warm, anywhere as long as it wasn't Colombia.

He had failed. His last shot had backfired and become a spectacular disaster, thanks to the work of the inhuman devil who had plagued him during the past several days. Cordero hadn't seen the big man at the ambush site, but he had no doubt that his nemesis was responsible for his ignominious fall.

There was no alternative but to flee for his life. The central committee of the cartel would have his head as soon as they found him.

The Medellín cartel had no patience with losers.

Fortunately Cordero had taken the precaution of stashing several million dollars in numbered accounts in Switzerland and Luxembourg. When he had finished running and was convinced that the trail behind him was cold and dead, there would be plenty of cash for him to draw on.

In the meantime there was a seaplane waiting on the other side of the bay. A short flight would wing the drug czar to safety in Nassau. After that, he'd be on the next flight to Europe. His first stop would be to a good plastic surgeon for some subtle alterations. Then the Colombian would disappear in some small town under one of his many secret identities. No one would ever connect him with the vanished Jaime Cordero.

Just in case he discovered that the cartel was on his trail, Cordero was taking the precaution of including some very valuable cartel documents among his escape kit. He had no doubt that he could trade the crime syndicate secrets for immunity and safety under the United States witness protection plan.

When it came to survival, Cordero had no loyalties.

BOLAN REACHED the rear door undetected. He smashed a glass panel by the handle and unlocked the door. The tinkle of glass was drowned out by the stutter of machine guns from the interior. A few of the Colombians had remained on the premises as a last line of defense. Bolan would have to do his best to avoid them.

The warrior prowled through the Early America dining room where he had entered, and crossed to the hall. A submachine gun hammered from the opposite room, although the gunner wasn't visible. A quick glance around the corner of the doorway showed that the broad hall ran the length of the building. Halfway down it widened into a two-story living room, which formed the bulge at the front of the house. The stairway to the second floor was invisible from where Bolan stood.

The warrior hesitated for a moment, wondering if he should take out the Colombians as he found them, or find Cordero and then get out.

His choices vanished when a shooter ran from his firing position into the corridor and turned down the hallway toward Bolan. The gunman raised his weapon, but the Executioner fired first, a burst that caught the Colombian in the chest and flung him hard onto his back.

The warrior spun around and nailed a second man as he popped through the door to see what the noise was about.

Bolan walked down the hall slowly, his M-16 out and probing for targets. He peered cautiously around the corner into the wide living room. Bullets kicked gouges in the tiles at his feet and chipped holes in the wall by his cheek.

The warrior pulled back fast. At least two men opposed him, one by the front door and the other on the upper-level balcony. He decided to go for them right away in case the rattle of firing from inside the house attracted more of the gunmen. After stepping back a few paces, he dashed for the living room, hit the ground rolling and came up behind a black marble coffee table.

He locked the M-16 on target on a gunman by the front door who had stood to get a better aim. The Executioner drilled him through the heart and shifted targets to the hardman upstairs.

Bolan and that gunman traded shots simultaneously. The shooter's bullets sang by Bolan's head, but the Executioner was rewarded, as the Colombian dropped his SMG and crashed through the railing.

The Executioner remained in place for a moment, warned by the sound of running feet that reinforcements were on the way. The front door crashed open and a man barged through, his Uzi up and questing.

The Colombian found Bolan the hard way as the M-16 slammed an explosive burst into the new arrival's face. The man crumpled to the door stoop, allowing the Executioner a clear shot at two more gunmen crowding the doorway.

Bolan stitched the pair with multiple bursts, forming a small barrier of dead bodies at the front entrance. He waited for more targets, but apparently no one else was willing to risk instant death by trying to force his way inside.

The warrior crept softly up the stairs, his ears cocked for the sounds of movement. He expected to find Cordero cowering somewhere on the upper floor. However, he didn't plan to underestimate the gangster, since a trapped animal could be dangerous, particularly one as vicious as Cordero.

He padded down the hall toward the far end of the house, probing carefully through each doorway. He'd decided to give the rooms a quick run-through before he went back and examined every hiding place carefully.

Bolan cursed when he poked through the door of the last bedroom along the hallway. A wall safe stood open and empty. Papers were strewn around the floor, indicating that someone was in a tremendous hurry. An open window and a chain ladder hooked onto the ledge proclaimed that Cordero had beaten a hasty retreat.

The warrior charged to the window, lifted his rifle and snapped off a shot at a figure scrambling down the staircase that led to the marina. Cordero vanished out of sight below the edge of the cliff.

The Executioner dropped the assault rifle and climbed out the window in pursuit, conscious of his vulnerability if one of the Colombian gunners spotted him hanging on the brightly lit side of the building.

Once on the ground he unleathered the Desert Eagle and pounded for the stairs. As he hit the first step, he heard the grumble of a powerful engine sputtering to life.

Bolan scrambled down as quickly as the slick treacherous stairs allowed. When he reached the foot of the steps Cordero was still visible, speeding for the opposite side of the bay in a sleek powerboat.

Bolan raced for a second craft that was moored at the dock. His only hope of catching the drug lord was if the keys had been left in the ignition. Luck was on his side. Cordero had been too panicked to throw the keys or sabotage the craft to foil anyone's attempt to follow. Bolan gunned the vessel into life.

Cordero had a long lead and a faster boat. He was far ahead and gaining a bigger lead with every second. A sliver of moon sparkling on the water made his boat visible in the distance. Bolan followed, steering in its foamy wake.

It looked as though Cordero was bound for Key Biscayne. He steered into one of the small inlets near a golf course, and the warrior turned to follow, trying to stay as close to the drug runner's path as possible. The last thing he needed was to rip out the bottom of his boat on a hidden shoal. Cordero knew he was being followed, and it was logical to assume that he would try anything to lose Bolan.

Bolan frowned as he caught sight of Cordero's goal—a Piper Cub floating on its pontoons, rocking gently in the swell. In a few moments the Colombian would be airborne and out of United States airspace.

Cordero slowed his craft and drifted to a stop beside the seaplane. He scrambled into the cockpit and seconds later the engine coughed to life. The plane began to slide over the water, heading for the open bay.

Bolan guided his speedboat to intercept. At their combined velocities the two crafts were closing the distance between them at breakneck speed.

Cordero held his course, aiming directly at the Executioner's boat. He was going to brave it out in the hope that he could reach takeoff velocity before the boat and plane crashed.

The warrior fisted the Desert Eagle, trying to aim the weapon as the boat pitched and yawed. He fired off several rounds as the gap closed, but couldn't tell if the shots were hitting home.

The aircraft suddenly veered off to one side and slowed, then headed for the shore. Bolan wondered if one of the .44 rounds had crippled the plane, but got his answer when Cordero slewed the machine around and headed out to sea again.

The warrior had already made his response, wrenching the boat into a wide turn to block the sweep to the outside. It would be a race to see who got there first.

The Executioner did.

Bolan maneuvered in front of the plane again. Cordero would have to run him down to get through to the ocean.

Cordero tried another tack, slowing the plane and zigzagging like a wide receiver trying to evade the safety.

Bolan made him pay for that strategy by slowing his own craft to improve the boat's stability and squeezing off another clip from the Desert Eagle.

This time he could see that the rounds had hit the target. The windscreen starred, and metal rang hollowly under the blows from the big Magnum slugs. A hole appeared in the engine cowling.

But the bullets hadn't struck anything vital. Cordero gunned the plane's engine and turned hard right, swinging past Bolan.

The warrior changed clips while he swung the wheel, maneuvering into position to get off a shot. Cordero was nearly beside him, presenting the Executioner with a perfect target.

The Desert Eagle misfired.

Bolan coaxed more power out of the boat and surged ahead, gaining steadily on the aircraft. One of the .44 slugs must have done more damage to the Piper than Bolan had thought, as Cordero seemed unable to urge the crippled aircraft to takeoff speed.

Foot by foot the warrior closed the gap. Cordero looked wildly around the cockpit, seeking an escape. But he had nowhere to run to.

Bolan dived over the side just as the speedboat smashed into one of the pontoons, crumpling the struts as though they'd been constructed of aluminum foil.

The impact ruptured the Piper's fuel tanks and the ensuing explosion consumed the two crafts. Liquid fire rained over the wreckage, and began to burn in a single funeral pyre for Cordero, incinerating the remains of the Colombian kingpin.

Bolan watched a few dozen yards distant, where he was treading water.

He was satisfied. It took an unusually savage killer to order the brutal murder of innocents simply to serve as a diversion for his real scheme to destroy the Mafia don. Finally, as if he had driven a stake through a vampire's heart, Bolan had put an end to the drug lord's machinations.

Bolan swam slowly toward Cordero's boat, which was floating a few hundred yards ahead of him.

Now it was time to turn his attention to Pinolla.

16

Bolan piloted the powerboat toward the distant Miami shore, heading for a point far removed from the Colombian headquarters. By now the estate would be swarming with police.

With Cordero eliminated, Pinolla would be feeling relaxed and cocky, and the Executioner could pick his time for the final showdown. He decided on one last probe of Pinolla's estate in case he could pick up any intelligence regarding the don's plan to consolidate drug distribution in the eastern United States.

He guided the boat up to the private dock of a darkened house. The owners would be surprised to find in the morning that they had acquired a powerboat overnight.

Bolan trudged quietly across the lawn to the road to flag down a taxi. Two vehicles slowed and then speeded up, obviously deciding that the big, disheveled man looked like trouble. A third taxi decided to chance the fare. The cab's first stop was a phone booth, where Bolan made a call to Wonderland.

"Striker," Brognola said dryly, "I heard that the Miami Funeral Directors Association has awarded you the keys to the city."

"It couldn't be helped, Hal. I should have things wrapped up in a few hours. Cordero's been taken out."

"That's good news. Thanks for the documents you dropped off. They'll pay big dividends. First off, it should be enough to revive the interstate agency we talked about."

"Great. I've got to go. I just wanted to let you know I'm alive."

"Stay hard, Striker."

A few minutes later the cab dropped Bolan at the gate of Pinolla's estate. The guards recognized him on sight and waved him through.

Bolan headed to the bunkhouse and opted for a quick shower to wash off the sticky salty residue before taking a look around. When he shut off the shower and stepped through the curtain he found himself looking down the barrels of three Uzis.

Behind the three enforcers stood the Fatman and several other gunmen. His eyes were as cold and hard as diamonds, but his cheeks were flushed.

"What's going on, boss?" Bolan asked. He eyed the distance between himself and the hardmen. No go. Any offensive move on his part would be suicide.

"Boss my ass," Pinolla hissed. "When I think of how you insinuated your way into my organization, it's all I can do to keep from killing you on the spot, Mr. Mack the Bastard Bolan."

Bolan swore to himself. In spite of all the precautions Pinolla had somehow learned his identity.

"Bolan?"

The Fatman smirked. "One of the Colombians you greased wasn't quite dead. He traded his life for a bit of information. He had recognized the guy who gunned him down from another encounter that he barely survived a couple of years earlier. I checked with a few other Mafia soldiers on the West Coast who had a run-in with the Executioner. The descriptions matched."

Pinolla shook his head in wonder at his own foolishness. "You really had me. I actually believed that Cordero screwed up when that bomb went off and almost killed us both. It must have been you who burgled my safe and slaughtered my boys in my study. You had it all planned, every step orchestrated to wipe me out. Now that Cordero is gone, I guess the Family was next on your hit list."

Bolan tensed to spring as Pinolla talked, planning to go for the first gunman and wrestle his SMG away from him. With a weapon he at least had a fighting chance.

The gunner stepped back before Bolan made his move. "You take an inch toward me," he said, "and your brains will be on the tiles."

Pinolla snapped his fingers and pointed to the door. "Take him outside."

"Can I get my clothes?"

Pinolla snorted in reply. He remembered the astonishing array of deadly gadgets Bolan had concealed on his person the first night he arrived. He threw Bolan a track suit.

Two men trained their weapons on the warrior as he dressed. Bolan realized that it would be a suicide play to try to take them out now. He resolved to travel the path of least resistance temporarily, make his break when the odds weren't stacked so heavily in the enemy's favor.

The two henchmen turned roughly and slammed him facefirst against the wall. His arms were jerked behind his back and his wrists were handcuffed together. One man hauled him around and pushed him forward, as the rest of the men closed ranks around him. The mafiosi weren't taking any chances with their valuable prisoner.

Pinolla stopped them before they left the barracks room. "I've got a real surprise for you, Bolan. The best specialist we have is flying in from Atlanta just to tend to you. They say he once kept a traitor alive for two months, and during that time he did something new and horrible to the guy every single day. I'm going to come and visit you all the time, Bolan, just to see for myself." Pinolla turned to his men. "Now get him out of here. And remember, anybody who damages him before he gets what he deserves will have to answer to me."

The guards shoved Bolan through the doorway. A limousine was waiting outside, and several armed men leaned against its fenders.

During the long drive the enforcers passed the time by speculating aloud about what the "doctor" would do to Bolan and providing graphic suggestions of what they'd inflict on the guy given the opportunity. Bolan turned his mind off from the grisly joking by trying to determine where he was being driven. As far as he could tell the limo was heading toward the Everglades.

When they finally reached their destination, the house was the sort of nondescript and charmless place he had expected. The limo drove into a long garage, and one of the gunners leaped out to tug down the door. The guards motioned Bolan from the car and escorted him through the inner garage door. They roughly prodded the big man into the first room along the hall and left him to cool his heels.

Bolan was in a bare room the size of a small cell. There were no windows, and a single low-wattage bulb cast a feeble light, adding to the gloomy surroundings. The only feature of the room besides the door was a small hole in the floor, which exuded a pungent reek. A grate in the door allowed an observer to check on the prisoner, but it was bolted on the outside.

The warrior examined the room carefully, checking for anything that could be loosened and used as a weapon. He gave up the quest after he had probed every inch, concluding that the only tools he would have to defeat his captors were his hands and his brain.

The floor was constructed of unfinished concrete—rough, hard and cold. Bolan could only sit for a few minutes before he had to get up and pace, realizing that he had to stay loose and alert.

Occasionally a face would appear at the grate in the iron door and stare at him for a few moments. Other than the mystery visitor he was left completely on his own.

After several hours footsteps echoed faintly down the hall. Bolan rose from the floor and stretched quickly. He'd already decided that if he was going to make a move to save himself he'd have to do it damn soon. Once he was in the hands of the Mafia torturer he was as good as dead, barring a miracle. After a few hours of the cruel treatment he would lose the physical ability to escape.

Bolan had seen the results of a turkey doctor's experiments on more than one occasion. There was no alternative but to kill someone who had been in his hands for a protracted period.

It was the only humane thing to do.

The warrior focused his energy for the forthcoming fight. The Mafia men had made a mistake handcuffing his wrists behind him. In order to strap him down they would have to release at least one wrist to bring his hands around in front. The Executioner would seize the moment.

The door banged open and a man wielding a pistol motioned him out. Three more gunmen crowded the hall, blocking both ends and covering Bolan with leveled weapons.

The warrior proceeded down the hall between his guards toward a doorway and a flight of steps that led to the upper floor. Faint sunlight filtered through a window on a landing halfway up, confirming that several hours had passed since his arrival. A prodding gun barrel directed Bolan through the open door.

He stepped into what appeared to be a small operating room. Various kinds of monitors flanked a hospital bed equipped with a complex array of straps and restraints. Bags of what seemed to be intravenous solutions stood near the head of the bed. An electroshock generator occupied one corner, beside an array of scalpels, pincers, vises, saws, pliers and other hideous instruments of torture. A hibachi sat on a table, ready for use.

A man in a white lab coat stood in the middle of the room, waiting for his victim. Tall and thin with faded light brown hair, he wore the sad expression of a funeral director.

"Welcome, Mr. Bolan. My name is Benson. I trust your visit with me will be long and unpleasant." He threw back his head and laughed, a shrill neighing sound. "My, he is a fine specimen," the man observed. "I shall have a great deal of pleasure with this subject."

He picked up a loaded syringe and stepped a little closer to Bolan. "I think that I shall start by tearing out his tongue," he said almost to himself. "He looks like a man of spirit and might try to commit suicide by biting through it. Hold him tight," the doctor ordered. "I'll inject him with this and when he's unconscious we can strap him to the bed."

Benson paused to squeeze a drop of fluid from the tip of the syringe.

Bolan's heart began to pound. He wouldn't get the chance he had thought he'd have after all. If that needle plunged into his arm it was game over. The warrior would wake up immobilized, kept alive by fluid dripping into his veins, monitored by the machines clustered around the bed—and with his tongue torn out.

Two of the guards holstered their weapons and grabbed him by the arms. Benson stepped closer, the needle leveled like a lance toward the warrior's arm.

Bolan lashed out with his powerful legs, connecting with the torturer's chest. The guy tumbled backward and crashed into a tray full of scalpels and probes. The instruments dropped to the floor with a clatter.

Bolan kicked backward with a foot and smashed one guard in the kneecap. The Mafia man dropped with a scream, clutching his injured leg. The Executioner shouldered the other guard, catching him unprepared and shoving him back into the other two hardmen.

Bolan raced for the door. He barreled up the stairs two at a time, put his head down when he came to the landing and smashed headfirst through the window.

He tumbled through like an acrobat and landed hard on the ground, winded. A second later he scrambled to his feet and sprinted to the back of the house.

A quick glance had revealed that the house had been built by the edge of a lake. How far the lake extended was impossible to determine from his angle. What was important was that a pair of swamp boats floated by the dock, craft that were designed to navigate the shallow waters of the Everglades. A powerful fan at the rear propelled the boat forward like a rock skipping over the water.

He sprinted for the boat, conscious that he had only a few moments to pull the keys from one of the boats and toss them into the water. He climbed aboard the second craft and fumbled awkwardly for the keys to the starter with his bound hands. The engine roared to life.

The noise of the fan attracted the mobsters, who had been searching the front of the house for him. Bolan shoved the boat into forward as one of the gunmen scooted behind the house, his weapon blazing as the boat pushed away from the dock.

When he reached a section of open water well out of range of the dock, Bolan slowed the craft momentarily and sat on the deck. With a little tugging, he was able to pull his legs through his bound hands. He was still chained, but at least he had more control over the boat.

It looked as if he would need it. The other boat sprang into life behind him. Evidently there had been a spare set of keys in the house.

Bolan headed farther into the swamp. He didn't have his bearings and had no idea of where he was headed. At the moment he wasn't concerned. Survival was top priority. Anything else was way down on the list.

The sun was now low in the sky. The Mafia men were well behind him but steady on his trail. Unless he lost them they'd follow until darkness made it impossible to see.

Bolan decided to take a moment for a quick inventory of the small craft to see if there was anything he could use against his pursuers. The boat was completely barren of potential weapons, but his search revealed a chilling fact: the gauge of the gas tank hovered just above empty. There was no way that he could outlast his pursuers.

He abruptly changed his plans and his course. Until now he had been steering over as much clear open water as he could find, conscious of the hazards that lurked below the smooth green surface of the water—anything from a sharp rock or water-soaked tree trunk to a lazy alligator.

He slowed and turned the swamp boat toward the shore. Trees heavy with Spanish moss hung low over the water, and rushes clogged the avenues between the trunks. Bolan throttled back and entered into a murky and oppressive world where the trees seemed to close in behind him.

He jumped for a branch a few feet above the water and levered himself up. His boat continued its slow, steady progress through the swamp.

The warrior had taken a calculated gamble. If he had remained on the boat it would have been only a matter of time until the gunners closed the gap and sniped at him from long distance. This way he had a fighting chance of surprising the pair as they negotiated between the trees.

Bolan crouched on a branch, knowing there was no guarantee that the Mafia men would follow his exact course in among the trees. However, he was betting on it since that would be the safest way for them to know that they remained on the right trail.

After minutes of tense waiting the warrior could hear the steady buzz of the approaching swamp boat. He readied himself to spring.

As the boat passed almost directly under his branch, the Executioner dropped onto the craft, his outstretched legs catching the shorter of the two men between the shoulders and propelling him into the stagnant water.

The other guy was as big as Bolan and had a tight grip on his Uzi machine pistol. He tried to twist around and line up a shot on Bolan, but the Executioner closed to striking distance first. He doubled his fists and dealt the guy a bruising blow to the jaw. Teeth and blood exploded from the gunner's mouth and he dropped his weapon in surprise, staggering backward.

Bolan followed and wrapped the handcuffs over the enforcer's head and around his throat, the metal chain biting into the guy's neck as he gasped in an attempt to take in air. Blood flowed over the cuffs as the wild struggles tore away the flesh from his muscular throat.

The gunman thrashed for a few more seconds then went limp.

Bolan dropped the corpse to the deck and checked the pockets, relieved to find the handcuffs key. The metal bracelets followed the Mafia man into the water.

The big man turned the drifting swamp boat in the direction of open water once more. Now that he'd taken care of the gangsters on his tail, he was able to think about getting back into the fight against Pinolla.

Bolan resolved to head back to the ranch where he'd been confined. He didn't know if he had killed the torturer, but he was more than a little curious to find out. He had a loathing for that kind of sick, twisted mind, and in this case there was a personal score to settle. Men in Benson's line of work deserved to be unemployed—permanently.

Fortunately Bolan had steered almost a straight course from the dock due west. He was able to double back, navigating by the rapidly sinking sun and a few landmarks he recognized from the trip out.

By the time he came in sight of the dock, the last rays of sunlight were fading behind him. He was able to coast in out of the sun, presenting a silhouette to anyone watching for him.

Only one man waited at the dock. He held his neck stiffly and turned his head slowly, probably injured during Bolan's escape. The big man throttled down to dock.

"Hey, Rodrigo, what happened to Joe?" the Mafia man called. "Where's Bolan?"

"Right here," Bolan replied as he lifted the Uzi and fired a burst.

The mobster spun and died when the 9 mm slugs bored through his chest. The sound of shots echoed around the small bay as Bolan jumped ashore.

He sprinted for the house. The back porch light snapped on and a man hobbled out, holding a cane in one hand and a large-caliber rifle in the other. "What the hell is going on out here?" he shouted into the darkness.

Bolan took the guy out on the run, then bounded up the steps and through the back door. He slowed his pace, knowing that anyone left in the house would be fully alert by now.

He padded through the kitchen and into the living room. Benson was leaning against the bar, a glass of whiskey in hand. His shirt was off and a large bandage was wrapped around his chest.

The torturer looked as though he were going to collapse when Bolan walked through the door unshackled and armed. He opened his mouth to plead but couldn't think of any lie or promise he could utter that might save his life.

Bolan leveled the Uzi and let loose a short burst that caught Benson in the chest. The guy fell to the floor, dead, his career of inflicting misery on his fellow man ended.

The warrior quit the house, snatching a Kevlar vest from the coatrack as he strode through the front door.

Pinolla was next at the top of the Executioner's hit list.

The Fatman was number one—with a bullet.

PINOLLA LISTENED to the telephone ring unanswered at the ranch. He'd lost count of how many times the phone had rung. He hadn't received any reports from the hideout other than the turkey doctor had arrived and would be starting work soon.

That had been hours ago.

A cold feeling washed over Pinolla. He didn't know for sure where Bolan was. With the almost legendary abilities that man possessed he could be outside Pinolla's gate right this minute.

The Fatman suddenly decided that he needed a change of scene.

17

Bolan guided his vehicle along a narrow country road that would eventually link up with a highway that led to Miami. The high beams of the Ford Escort he'd liberated from the ranch carved through the pitch-black night as he pushed the car to the maximum safe speed on the bumpy, potholed tarmac.

During his cursory search of the ranch he'd uncovered a small cache of 9 mm ammunition to complement the Uzis he had recovered from the dead mafiosi. It seemed somehow fitting that bullets purchased with the Fatman's tainted blood money would be the cause of his demise.

When Bolan reached North Miami, he tried to phone Pinolla to establish whether he was still at the estate. His attempts to deliver an urgent message failed. Whoever was answering the phone wasn't giving out even the smallest clue as to Pinolla's whereabouts.

The warrior wasn't surprised. Pinolla had been caught with his pants down too many times already. Bolan had played him like a trout and the mobster had gobbled the bait.

Bolan wasn't about to take no for an answer. A few minutes later he drove past the Fatman's estate. Every light on the grounds blazed, and the hired security men at the gate had been replaced by hardened enforcers, holding their subguns in plain sight. Their eyes warily scanned every car that cruised by. With Bolan on the loose any little thing out of the ordinary was suspect.

Bolan surmised that by now Pinolla had learned of his miraculous escape and the enemy gunners were at full alert and waiting for his arrival.

His assault would now be significantly more difficult to pull off, but Bolan had no intention of backing off. He had gone through too much to allow Pinolla to escape at the final moment.

In essence this phase wasn't much different from his assault on Cordero's headquarters. Bolan pulled into a parking spot a block away and trotted back to Pinolla's place. He carried an Uzi under his jacket, and several spare clips had been crammed into a pocket. He had also been able to scrounge a knife, which he wore strapped at his waist.

Bolan cut through the back of an adjacent property, following the shoreline of a small lake that each of the estates fronted. Just before he reached Pinolla's home, he climbed a tree to gain a view from another angle.

The prospect wasn't encouraging. The Fatman must have called on every soldier in the Family to come to his aid. Several pairs of men walked their beats along the low wall that edged the grounds, and Bolan detected a few gunmen hiding in the shadows of the outbuildings. No doubt there were more tucked away ready to ambush intruders.

Bolan crouch-walked to the wall that separated the estates. He pressed himself against its base and waited for a pair of guards to pass. He could hear their feet thudding on a small path that Pinolla had had installed so that his sentries wouldn't damage the lawn.

The voices of the Mafia men drifted to the warrior on the evening breeze.

"Pullin' this job pisses me off," one guy complained. "Here we are waitin' for Dr. Death to show up, and Pinolla buggers off to Orlando. At least he could've hung around to see how it goes down."

"Yeah, well, he's the boss. He says jump, we jump. I don't blame him for takin' off. Let me tell you what I heard about this guy Bolan...."

The voices faded as the men continued on.

Bolan smiled, grateful that the Fates had put him in this place at this time. Pinolla's plan had almost worked. The Executioner had nearly been decoyed into an attack on an empty cage.

He trotted back through the trees toward the car. Brognola had given him the address of a known Mafia safehouse in Orlando, and in a few hours the Fatman was going to get the surprise of his life.

PINOLLA RESISTED the temptation to telephone the estate one more time. He had already called twice from his car phone while en route to Orlando.

The Fatman sipped at a glass of bourbon, telling himself that his men would let him know what happened. He put down the drink and started to pace the master bedroom restlessly, conscious that he had already had three stiff belts.

He had retired to the safety of his top-floor condo after sending his wife and sons on a quick trip to the Caribbean. The retreat was modest by the standards of his Miami estate, only three bedrooms, but was lavishly furnished in the old-money style he cultivated.

Only six guards had accompanied the don, most of whom sat playing poker in the living room. He had preferred to leave everyone else to face Bolan, praying that the large force would accomplish what no one else had so far—take down the Executioner.

Pinolla strode to the window and stared out at the city lights, wishing once again that the phone would ring and give him the news that he longed to hear: Mack Bolan was dead.

A few hours ago it had seemed that anything was possible. Once he had eliminated Bolan he'd have been a hero among the Families, the man who ended Bolan's savage and destructive war against the Mafia.

The Commission would have heaped honors on his head, maybe even made him the first among equals, the king of kings. At the very least, every Family in the country would have been deeply in his debt for plucking out the greatest thorn in their side.

Now Bolan was loose. Pinolla mentally kicked himself for his overconfidence. He had thought that Bolan was beaten, as good as dead, once he had been delivered to the ranch.

Another big mistake he had to add to the others.

Now he had lost contact with the ranch, and that could mean only one thing where Bolan was concerned.

From the perspective of what he knew now, it was easy to see how the clever and persuasive Mack Bolan had led him around like a sheep. But this time Pinolla had turned the tables and outsmarted Bolan.

The Fatman knew the Executioner's reputation and had arranged to use his own character against him. Bolan's aggressive, unrelenting nature would lead him into a trap prepared for his destruction. Pinolla had commandeered every man in his organization who could still hold a gun. Bolan would be outnumbered by more guns than he had demonstrated that he could handle.

Pinolla glanced at his watch. If he hadn't gotten a favorable report from the estate within the next two hours, he'd head for the airport. A couple hours later he'd be beyond the reach of both Bolan and the law. He regretted having to leave, but Pinolla didn't plan to set foot on United States soil again until the Executioner was dead.

The Fatman felt the tension burning in his chest. He drained his glass and reached for the telephone once again.

BOLAN STOLE PAST the bored-looking security guard and took an elevator to the thirty-third floor, which was the penthouse. He stepped from the car, his Uzi up and probing. Anyone who happened to be in the hall would get a shock, but Bolan considered the odds of his running into a Mafia gunner and decided that being shocked was better than being dead.

He strode to Pinolla's unit and paused outside the door. Several voices penetrated the veneer, telling him that perhaps four men were inside.

Bolan raised his boot to kick down the door, but hesitated when his eyes caught an exit sign at the end of the hall.

He paced down the corridor and through the exit, then ran up the few stairs to the roof. A powerful blast of air slammed into him as the wind pulled at his jacket.

The warrior moved to the edge of the roof and stared down at the broad balconies lining the sides of the building. He figured that one of them would serve as a safer point of entry than if he barged through the front door into an unknown number of gun sights.

He jogged along the roof until he had counted approximately the number of steps he had measured on the floor below. The balcony directly over the side should enter into Pinolla's living room. A metal roof covered the balcony, so Bolan couldn't tell if doors leading onto it were open or shut.

Bolan tied an end of his rope around a vent, slung the Uzi and slid over the side of the building. It was a short hand-over-hand climb to the balcony below, although skirting the metal roof without making noise proved a little tricky.

The Executioner stepped onto the balcony and readied his weapon. Through a gap in the draperies he could see two men smoking and laughing. A pile of cards lay scattered on a table between them, and each wore a pistol in a shoulder holster. An Ingram MAC-10 lay near the cards. He could see the shadow of one more man in the kitchen, which adjoined the living room, but saw no sign of the Fatman.

Suddenly one of the men at the table looked up, warned by some sixth sense that he was being watched. He spotted Bolan's shadowy figure outside the sliding glass doors and dived for the Ingram, shouting a warning to his companions.

The Executioner reacted with lightning reflexes, triggering a deadly stream of slugs through the glass and into the living room.

The man who had shouted died before he reached his Ingram, skewered by shards of glass and half a dozen 9 mm slugs.

The Executioner tracked onto the other card player. The chair rocketed backward and the Mafia man spilled onto the Persian carpet as Bolan tagged him with a blast that destroyed his ribs.

Bolan charged through the shattered glass door and dropped behind an overstuffed couch. The gunner in the kitchen fired a burst, hitting the couch and filling the air above Bolan's head with fragments of pulped foam. The warrior edged around the couch and returned fire.

More shots buzzed above his head, this time coming at him from the hallway. Bolan triggered a burst in return and the gunner jerked back out of sight.

The Executioner frowned. He was caught in a cross fire, but at least no one would be leaving the condo through the front door. Anyone who tried that exit was a dead man. Bolan would see to that.

PINOLLA SUPPRESSED an urge to scream when shooting erupted down the hall. He sat paralyzed by fear for long seconds before his head cleared enough to think straight.

It had to be Bolan. The man was superhuman. Instead of falling into Pinolla's carefully set trap, the Executioner had tracked him down to the one place where Pinolla thought he was safe.

The mobster choked down the bile rising in his throat and stood. He hadn't stayed alive as long as he had without being a careful man. Other killers had tried to hit him, but he was still alive and kicking. There was a trick or two left in the Fatman.

He pulled open a drawer in a bedside table and flicked a concealed switch. A section of mirrored tiles sprang an inch away from the wall—a secret exit that not even his wife knew about, saved for a dire emergency.

That day had arrived in spades.

Pinolla wedged his fingers into the opening and pulled, revealing a door. He stepped through and carefully pulled the hinged section of mirrored wall shut behind him. He slammed the connecting door and stood inside a closet on the other side of the wall. The Mafia kingpin ran from the closet, through the sparsely furnished apartment beyond and out into the hall.

He dashed down the hall for the bank of elevators, gasping, his heart pounding from the unaccustomed exertion. The sounds of gunfire echoed in the hall, growing fainter as he made his escape.

Pinolla pounded the button to summon the lift as he looked down the hall, terrified that at any moment Bolan might burst through the condo door, gun in hand, hot for his blood.

The elevator doors slid silently open and the mobster stumbled through. Two hardmen and his driver waited downstairs, another precaution he was glad he had taken. Pinolla's breathing steadied as the car descended. He just might get out of this alive.

SLUGS SKIMMED over Bolan's head, smashing the crystal lamps behind him and plunging the living room into darkness. He concentrated on muzzle-flashes of the gunner in the kitchen in order to nullify the threat of gunfire coming from two sides. He sighted on the next wink of the hardman's SMG and fired controlled bursts. He could hear the slugs thudding ineffectually into metal surfaces beyond the gunner. Finally the Executioner was rewarded with an agonized scream that informed him that he'd scored.

The warrior shifted targets, first changing clips. He started to crawl down the length of the sofa, a safe course of action now that the second mafioso was out of commission.

The man in the hallway had lost track of Bolan, since the bulky piece of furniture screened the warrior from sight. Bolan poked the Uzi around the edge of the couch, angling the barrel under an end table, and sighted on the corridor where the enemy gunman crouched.

The hardman had disappeared. Now it was a game of cat and mouse between the two men as they tracked each other among the furniture.

The warrior sat and listened for a moment. The apartment was completely silent.

Suddenly a spring in the couch gave a tiny squeak.

Bolan moved almost on automatic, realizing that the gunman was just above him. He bolted for the end of the couch, rose and swung around to catch the guy in his sights.

The gunner fired first as Bolan stood to shoot. Most of the bullets screamed by Bolan's chest, but a couple of lucky shots smashed into the Uzi, rendering it useless. The warrior was fortunate to merely suffer stinging hands from the impact.

Bolan flung away the Uzi, and followed the gun with a dive. Another burst passed harmlessly over his back. An instant later he smashed into the gunner, catching him above the knees. Both men tumbled off the couch onto the floor.

The mafioso had dropped his gun, so the two men fought it out on the carpet. The Italian was tall and strong, at least a match for Bolan, and all hard muscle.

Bolan smashed hard at his chest and kidneys with a rocklike fist. His adversary groaned in pain, but returned blow for blow with hammer force. The Mafia hardman tried to knee Bolan in the groin, but the warrior blocked that move and delivered a solid blow to the guy's jaw. The mafioso spit blood in Bolan's face.

The Executioner reached for his knife when he had an opening. The hardman butted Bolan in the forehead and the knife skidded away into the darkness.

Bolan dropped knees first on the enforcer, exploding the air from his lungs. He wrapped his hands around the other man's neck and squeezed hard.

In a last burst of energy the enemy pulled up a knee between them and managed to break Bolan's hold. The mobster staggered to his feet, hurting, but with plenty of fight still in him. The fighters faced each other, prepared to continue the battle, when the overhead light came on and a voice from behind penetrated their concentration. A slim man stood in the hall, training his subgun on the combatants. "Well, well," he said. "Two birds with one stone—Bolan, and you, Carmen, the bastard who's been jumping my wife. This is my chance to finally get rid of you, no muss, no fuss. Say goodbye! I'll be the hero this time instead of the goat."

He squeezed the trigger just as Bolan took advantage of the momentary distraction to send Carmen flying with a kick to the chest. Carmen absorbed the burst intended for both of them, and crashed into his traitorous companion, dead on his feet.

Bolan crossed the few feet to the hallway in a second, and liberated the wronged husband's subgun. After making sure the guy would be out cold for a while, he hefted the Ingram and walked cautiously down the hall.

Now nothing stood between him and the Fatman.

18

A closed door blocked the end of the hall, and Bolan opened it with a .45-caliber key. The big man applied a heavy boot to the shattered wood, and the riddled door slammed back into the wall.

Bent in a combat crouch, Bolan crept inside, the Ingram tracking back and forth. The room was dark, with only a faint glow penetrating thick red drapes. He reached up and snapped on a light switch without taking his eyes from his surroundings.

The room was deserted. He searched the bedroom and the adjoining bath, even examined the ceiling to try to discern a trapdoor large enough for Fatman. He concluded that Pinolla had somehow given him the slip. Bolan pounded his fist on the wall in frustration, and one of the mirror tiles cracked. Shards of mirror tinkled to the floor.

The warrior cursed as he looked at the broken glass. The edge of a concealed exit was visible where the tiles had broken away.

After Bolan directed a few rounds near the edge of the hidden door, a catch released and the exit popped open. In moments he was making his way through the adjacent condo. He had to give the Fatman credit for a brilliant evasion.

The warrior streaked for the elevator and pounded the button. He was aboard a car and descending after a brief wait. As it dropped, Bolan could only hope that he wasn't too late.

He got off at the level marked for parking and sprinted to the garage exit. He shoved a ten-dollar bill through the slot in the Plexiglas window and asked the kid on duty if he'd seen a limo leave in the past five minutes.

The kid raised his eyes from his comic book. "Maybe. I'm not sure." He had that crafty look that indicated he did know something—if the price was right.

Bolan dug another ten from a wallet he had lifted back at the chicken ranch and handed it over to the junior extortionist.

"Yes, sir. One left about two minutes ago. It turned left and then right at the traffic lights. The driver seemed to be in a hell of a hurry."

The warrior jogged the short distance to where he'd parked the Escort and sped after Pinolla with a squeal of rubber.

Bolan followed the directions and shortly came to the entrance ramps for I-4. The warrior had to gamble now. It was equally likely that Pinolla had fled north or south along the interstate or had simply kept driving through Orlando.

Bolan tried to place himself in the Fatman's shoes. If he was scared and running for his life, which way would he go? The big man guessed that he'd head south to try to shake pursuit and yet arrive back within the protection of his armed enclave.

He steered the car onto the southbound ramp and accelerated as soon as he reached the highway. If he had guessed wrong he'd find out soon enough.

In minutes he caught sight of a large black car far down the straightaway, just the right size to be a stretch limo.

THE CAR PHONE RANG, making Pinolla jump. He picked it up and put it to his ear. "Can we outrun him?" he asked. The answer didn't please him, and the don slammed down the receiver.

"There's a car coming up fast behind us. Maybe it's just some crazy driver, but I think it's Bolan. He's found me somehow. We can't escape him because we'll be out of gas in thirty miles at top speed." He glared at the bodyguards as though it were their fault, forgetting momentarily that he had forbidden the driver to stop for gas on the way to Orlando in his haste to reach a safe haven.

Pinolla's wavering confidence vanished like a bursting bubble. He had imagined that he was safe, at least until he went to ground somewhere else. The Mafia don realized that he would never be safe again as long as the Executioner dogged his trail.

"Let him come," one of the bodyguards urged. "As soon as he pulls up beside us, we blast him or at least cripple his car."

Pinolla ignored the enforcers. The guy didn't know what the hell he was talking about. The Mafia don didn't think his men stood much of a chance against the Executioner.

He had a horrible vision of the limo cartwheeling through the air as flames shot from the body, crushing and crippling the passengers before it came to rest and barbecued the survivors.

Pinolla wasn't about to risk it. He had a better idea. He dialed the driver and ordered him to head for Adventure

World, an amusement park a few miles ahead that the Fatman owned a piece of.

He had often entertained himself by wandering through the park behind the scenes, especially through the maze of tunnels that honeycombed the property. He could lose Bolan underground and could escape under cover of the crowds the next day.

With luck, he might even have an opportunity to execute the Executioner.

BOLAN SAW THE LIMO accelerate as he steered around a banked curve. The distance between the vehicles increased as the larger car shot ahead. He hadn't been able to approach close enough to read the license plate, but he was convinced he was hunting the right quarry.

The warrior knew that his compact could barely keep up with the powerful engine in the other car, and he was bound to lose Pinolla over a long pursuit.

The limousine switched lanes abruptly, earning an angry blast from another vehicle it cut off. The black car roared down an exit ramp, and Bolan twisted his wheel to follow.

The two cars played follow the leader down access roads for the next ten minutes as the limo driver tried to shake the Executioner. Bolan stuck like gum to a shoe, closing the gap a little at every turn.

Tiring of the game, the stretch limo accelerated at maximum speed and turned down a drive leading to Adventure World, a well-known amusement park.

The warrior followed, knowing it was a one-way trip, since the long drive toward the parking lot clearly indicated that there was no through access. Once Pinolla reached the park, he'd have to make a stand.

The limousine screeched to a halt beside the main gate. Pinolla climbed out and ran for the interior of the park, flashing something to the security guards stationed at the gate. His bodyguards and the driver leaped out of the limo and leveled their weapons as Bolan rushed at them in his sedan.

The amusement park security guards scrambled for cover when the Mafia enforcers fisted their guns.

Bolan wasn't inclined to participate in a gunfight at the moment. The bodyguards could delay him for a significant amount of time while Pinolla crawled down some rat hole.

The limo was parked in front of a chain link fence that swung back when the park was open, and Pinolla had raced through the gate. Beyond the fence stood a line of turnstiles that led to the main entrance to the park, a smiling clown face forty feet high. People wandered up his long tongue and through his open, smiling mouth to the attractions inside.

Bolan drove the sedan right for the fence, ignoring the gunmen, who opened fire from long range. Few of their bullets struck the vehicle with Bolan swerving to spoil their aim. As the range closed, bullets slammed into the passenger side and fractured the windows into tiny glass cubes.

In seconds Bolan had run the gauntlet and broken through the chain fence. The rear window of his Escort dissolved as the Mafia gunners swung to follow the moving target.

He crushed the brake pedal to the floor, sending the car skidding into the turnstiles. The Escort stopped with a wrench as the entry gates sheared away with a screech of tortured metal.

Bolan popped the seat belt and swung around to face the opposition, his Ingram locking on target as he turned.

He was behind the gunners, having outflanked them by sheer brute mobility. The Executioner aimed over the back of the front seat and drilled a burst that slammed into the chest of one of the enforcers.

He shifted and acquired another man in his sights. Bolan cored the machine gunner with a stream of slugs that stitched the guy from crotch to throat, leaving him crumpled on the ground, leaking red.

The third man had sought cover. Bolan searched the area around the limousine as best he could, but his field of view was too restricted by the car frame to allow him to inspect his surroundings fully.

Bolan eased into the back seat. The hidden gunner could spring up anywhere, which made the warrior's car a potential death trap.

Something clinked softly to his left. Bolan turned away from the sound, wondering if he was being decoyed by a pebble or an item thrown to distract him. That was the kind of ploy the warrior would have used in a similar situation. When his enemy's nerves were drawn as taut as a bowstring, the Executioner could sometimes spook him with a simple diversion.

When the sound was repeated, Bolan swung back, confident that he wasn't being foxed.

The Mafia enforcer sprang up beside the ventilated passenger window like a pop-up toy and sprayed the front seat where the warrior had been sitting, hosing the interior with a stuttering death stream.

The Executioner answered the volley of slugs with a blast from the back seat.

Bolan inserted a fresh clip as the echoes of gunshots bounced back from the grinning clown face.

Now there was no one between Joey "Fatman" Pinolla and the Executioner.

PINOLLA STUMBLED AHEAD as his breath came in ragged gasps. He ground to a halt, knowing that he couldn't run another step, even if Bolan was two feet behind him.

He rested for a moment, then began to walk slowly down the main street of the amusement village, which was lined with shops and small restaurants that normally presented a delightful way for visitors to part with a bit of spare cash.

At the foot of the street a mountain constructed of steel girders rose to an eight-story height, and beyond it lay his destination, the Castle, the centerpiece of the horror village.

The mobster picked up his pace a little as he hastened toward the Castle. If Bolan wanted to get him, Pinolla wouldn't make it easy.

BOLAN STARED down the street, looking past the long line of shops that ran to the foot of a mountain. Antique streetlights illuminated the shopping village with a cheerful tone. Dolls, T-shirts and handicrafts filled the windows, would-be tangible memories of carefree fun.

Bolan was caught between a rock and a hard place. On the one hand he needed to press the pursuit of the mobster to prevent him from going to ground in one of the many hiding spots in the park. However, boldness might just get the warrior a bullet in the back as he plunged through unknown territory.

Presumably the Fatman had picked this place to make his stand with something special in mind. He would be sure to have a surprise in store for the Executioner when he closed in for the kill.

Bolan shoved the idea from his mind. He'd trust to skill and a little luck to snatch victory from even the grimmest circumstances.

He edged warily forward, scanning the shadows in every doorway and looking quickly to see if the doors had been disturbed. There was an almost infinite number of dim, shadowy places for a man to hide. The amusement park was silent, as though Bolan were the only man alive on earth.

At the end of the shops he was faced with a choice. Signs pointed in opposite directions, indicating Pioneerland and Futureland. A third post pointed directly ahead to Mysteryland. As a final choice he could climb a broad path that twisted to the top of the mountain.

A clatter sounded to his left, from what appeared to be a tunnel that led under the mountain. Bolan jogged inside, his finger snug against the trigger of the Ingram. A few feet inside the passageway, clever scene setting tried to persuade him that he was entering a coal mine.

"Don't shoot!" a voice tinged with terror yelled from the darkness.

Bolan relaxed a little. A man in a park maintenance uniform stood at the junction to a side tunnel. He was piloting a small electric cart piled with tins of paint. The young man shook as he stared down the muzzle of the submachine gun.

"Where did he go?" Bolan barked.

"That way, down to the Castle."

Bolan gestured with the gun and the young man took the hint, running like a jackrabbit for the gate.

The big man trotted through the tunnel and emerged into what appeared to be a cemetery, crammed with gravestones inscribed with witty epitaphs. The Castle stood in front of him, designed as a cold and forbidding ruin. Spiky towers loomed against the night sky. The Mummy's Tomb and Aladdin's Journey eerily flanked the castle; a wolf howled mournfully from somewhere beyond the haunted house.

Bolan marched the grave-lined path to the castle, where Abandon Hope All Ye Who Enter Here was inscribed on a sign above the lintel. The warrior opened the squeaky door and stepped into a wide atrium. A large chandelier draped with cobwebs hung from the high ceiling, and the walls showcased portraits of evil-looking individuals. A sign directed visitors through a side door to the Chamber of Horrors, warning that it wasn't suitable for the easily frightened. A slideway, stationary now, led into the interior of the house.

The normally spooky effect was dissipated by bright lights to facilitate maintenance and an absence of special effects or movement. None of the mysterious magic clung to the static, rather garish displays.

Bolan walked into the Chamber of Horrors, which was rather mild compared to some of the cruelties inflicted on people in real life. He ignored the overpainted displays, searching the crannies of the exhibit for Pinolla. The bright lights showed details not normally visible to the public, such as emergency exits and employees' entrances. Bolan suspected that Pinolla remained concealed behind one of these innocuous doors.

Suddenly the lights dimmed, and the room was filled with wails and shrieks of agony as the animated figures lumbered into life. Directly in front of the Executioner a realistic simulation of a long-haired woman writhed in flames as two priests prayed over her in a reproduction of an auto-da-fé.

He retreated through the screams into the great hall. The slideway had clanked into motion and flowed like a black band around the corner and out of sight. Groans and metallic thumps echoed down the hall as flickering lights cast a weird and wavering glow.

At least Bolan was certain that he'd come to the right place. Somewhere inside, the Fatman was waiting for him. The events of the past few days had boiled down to a final confrontation between the Mafia kingpin and the Executioner.

Bolan stepped onto the slideway and peered into the gloom, trying to ignore the distractions of sound and light as he pointed the Ingram down the corridor in quest of Pinolla's blood.

THE DON WATCHED a closed-circuit monitor as the Executioner stepped onto the slideway. The entire park was riddled with cameras to keep an eye on what was going on at all times. From his control console the Fatman could observe every move the Executioner made. When Bolan reached the place Pinolla had selected . . .

One of the many monitors showed the warrior passing a checkpoint not far from the assassination point. Pinolla hastened to take his firing position.

It was such a fitting place to die.

The mobster crouched by a mock door made from flexible plastic. A lever on a cam pushed the door out while a machine behind him groaned and growled menacingly. A bright green light bathed the small enclosure.

The Fatman steadied his pistol with both hands and waited. Seconds later Bolan came into view, crouching and tracking the Ingram from side to side.

Pinolla stifled a giggle as he sighted on the middle of Bolan's back, just above the big man's heart. It was payback time, and the Mafia don squeezed the trigger.

Bolan pitched forward on the slideway and was carried out of sight. Pinolla jumped to his feet with a triumphant yell, waving his pistol in the air.

Killing Bolan had been such a pleasure that Pinolla was sorry it had happened so quickly. The Fatman laughed aloud, the sound momentarily besting the groans that surrounded him.

19

Bolan lay stunned by the hammer blow to his back. He rolled over slowly, his eyes searching the darkness for traces of the hidden shooter. His back throbbed painfully, and he could almost feel the bruise spreading from the point of impact. He was grateful that he had taken the time to don the Kevlar flak jacket he'd grabbed at the ranch. Otherwise the lethal slug would have blown his heart through his chest.

The slideway carried him down a narrow corridor where eyes glowed at him fiercely from all angles. Doors buckled and bulged as though something strong and evil locked inside were trying to escape.

The ride swept into an area where a ghostly band climbed from their coffins and played a dead man's march. Spectral shadows and witches whirled overhead among bats and ravens.

Bolan climbed to his feet and walked back against the flow of the slide. He had noticed an access point into the restricted areas, concealed behind a red neon devil.

He shot open the door and stepped into a brightly lit corridor that paralleled the ride. The cacophony of horrific noises faded somewhat as the door swung shut, replaced by mechanical grunts from the automated machinery. Status boards along the hallway informed staff of the condition of the displays.

After a couple of false starts that led nowhere, he noticed a sign that pointed the direction to the control room. Bolan hefted the MAC-10 and trotted down the pathway.

Pinolla was about to see the Executioner rise from the dead.

THE FATMAN STROLLED leisurely back to the control room. He planned to summon a car from Miami to pick him up and take him back to his base. Until it arrived, he'd spend the time watching Bolan's body make the circuit of the attraction.

Pinolla had already decided that he'd take the Executioner's remains back with him. He knew an excellent taxidermist back in Miami, and was toying with the idea of paying the guy a visit. Stuffed and mounted for display, the Executioner would cause a sensation among the Fatman's Mafia friends.

As he walked into the control room, a chime and a flashing light announced trouble. Someone had entered the areas closed to the public. Pinolla checked the monitors with mounting anxiety. Hidden cameras should have shown Bolan sprawled dead on the slideway. Instead, the screens showed no trace of the big man.

The Mafia chief wasn't about to hang around. His best shot hadn't finished the Executioner, and he didn't have the stomach to try again. The warrior seemed to be invulnerable.

BOLAN SLIPPED into the control room, a quick glance revealing that it was deserted. The flickering images on the monitors made it painfully obvious how easy it had been for Pinolla to ambush him.

An image attracted his attention. He saw Pinolla open an access door in the Chamber of Horrors and disappear from view. Bolan snatched a key labeled Master from a rack and trotted after the mafioso.

He emerged into the grotesque animated torture chamber, strode past a bloody guillotine with an executioner displaying a newly severed head and unlocked the door where Pinolla had vanished. A long stairway descended into the earth, the sounds of heavy machinery vibrating up the well.

Bolan bounded down the stairs two at a time. The Mafia chief had a significant head start and the warrior would have to scramble to catch up.

A corridor ran into the distance at the end of the stairs, each side lined with closed, locked doors. Fluorescent lights glowed overhead. Bolan could have been deep within the bowels of any large hospital or office building.

The warrior proceeded down the corridor. The environment was a tremendous improvement over the horror house, where he had been unable to see or hear clearly because of the noise and distractions. A T-junction branched off down similar halls, and the Executioner paused. Pinolla's plan was obviously to lose him among the labyrinth of tunnels. He shrugged and turned left, dropping to the ground immediately as a bullet skimmed by his cheek. Pinolla stood in the mouth of a tunnel up ahead, a pistol in his hand.

The Executioner replied with a burst that tore concrete chips out of the walls. The don raced out of sight.

The warrior rose and pursued. He paused at the side tunnel, expecting a blast when he poked around the edge. The corridor was empty, but he heard terrified screaming emanating from a room at the end.

"I know you're out there, Bolan," Pinolla shouted, a quaver in his voice. "I've got a hostage, and I'm going to blow her brains out unless you let me and this woman walk out of here. Tell him, lady!" A woman's shriek emphasized his words.

Bolan looked warily around the corner. Pinolla had his arm around the neck of a woman in her forties, his pistol resting against her temple. A companion hid under a table in a corner. Fabric lay cluttered around the sewing room.

"I don't have much patience, Bolan. If you're going to kill me I might as well take a few people with me. What's it going to be?"

Bolan only hesitated a moment. The Ingram was a fine weapon for its class, but Bolan had no intention of trusting it for the pinpoint accuracy required to kill Pinolla before the don could squeeze the trigger and obliterate his hostage.

The big man stepped into the doorway, his weapon trained on Pinolla.

The Fatman motioned Bolan into the room while he backed away.

"Drop the gun and kick it over to me," Pinolla ordered.

Bolan did as he was told, all the while looking for an opportunity to jump the mobster. The Executioner finally gave it up. There was nothing he could do without endangering the woman's life.

The two men circled the room until Pinolla reached the door with the seamstress in tow. "Don't get any smart ideas about following me," he warned Bolan, "or the bitch gets it. Understand?"

Bolan nodded, and Pinolla extended his right leg to toe the Ingram out of sight. Then the Mafia man backed out of the door, dragging his hostage with him.

The Executioner waited until he thought that Pinolla was out of sight. The woman in the corner continued to sob, and muttered to herself in a language Bolan didn't understand. He took a moment to dump out the contents of a purse that sat on a stool and extracted a small hand mirror.

Bolan didn't really believe the Mafia lord's threat to shoot the woman as soon as he spotted the Executioner. Pinolla would have nothing to gain and a lot to lose by canceling his own insurance. However, desperate men were unpredictable, and the warrior preferred not to risk a confrontation with an innocent life hanging in the balance.

He dropped to his knees and poked the mirror around the edge of the door just above the floor. The tiny image showed that Pinolla had dragged his captive beyond view.

Bolan dashed to the next corner, pausing momentarily to examine a spot of blood on the floor. Pinolla had been hit earlier and was leaving a trail that a pursuer couldn't miss.

The warrior followed the pair for another few turns using his mirror to ensure he didn't run up Pinolla's back, guided by the faint drops of red marring the immaculate halls. The mobster might have known where he was going, but there didn't appear to be rhyme or reason to the numerous twists and turns the crime boss took.

Pinolla must have believed that he could shake Bolan simply by following a convoluted path. Bolan journeyed past laundry rooms, storage and costuming centers, lounges, boiler rooms and a hundred other facilities. A whole world as complex as the park above existed below the surface.

Fortunately the underground kingdom appeared deserted. Bolan hadn't seen a sign of anyone other than the unlucky seamstresses.

The warrior could hear Pinolla and his captive slowly plodding ahead. He hung back, confident that Pinolla couldn't give him the slip now.

A muffled thump was followed by a sound that resembled a sack of potatoes dropping to the floor. Bolan checked around the corner and saw Pinolla slither through a door in the wall. The woman was slumped on the floor.

The warrior rushed forward and checked the woman over quickly. A lump seeped blood into her hair and she lay unconscious, but otherwise she appeared unhurt.

Using the master, he unlocked the door through which Pinolla had passed, then climbed a flight of stairs. A sign on the exit door reminded characters to check their costumes. Bolan pulled open the door and stepped into an old-fashioned fun house. A mirror opposite the door stretched the big man until he appeared about eleven feet high.

The warrior had to proceed cautiously. He was unarmed, easy prey to a long-distance shot from Pinolla's .45. The Executioner would have to close to arm's length before he could attempt to take out the don.

Bolan spotted a staff door and sped through. He had an idea that he could reverse the stunt Pinolla had pulled on him at the Castle. As he entered the control center, Pinolla was visible on the monitor, moving slowly in what appeared to be unfamiliar surroundings.

The big man flipped on the master control switch and the fun house, until then silent and static, came alive with jolly carnival music. Animated figures popped from hidden receptacles or danced to mechanical prompts. The lights dimmed to provide minimal illumination.

Bolan watched Pinolla jump back, startled as the head of a mechanical dragon popped from behind a papier-mâché mountain and roared. The mobster moved forward cautiously, knowing that he was no longer alone.

The warrior trotted from the control room, a small diagram posted on the back of the door telling him where he was and where he wanted to be. Moments later Bolan stood at the edge of the hall of mirrors, waiting for Pinolla to enter.

The Executioner strode forward and came face-to-face with a short, squat image of himself, followed by another in which he seemed to wear angel's wings. A hologram of a fiery devil stood beside him as he turned the corner of the maze of mirrors.

Another step brought him face-to-face with Pinolla.

The Fatman raised his pistol and fired, smashing the reflection of Bolan into shards.

Pinolla turned and fired two more rounds, shattering silvered surfaces in a cascade of geometric fragments. The sound of breaking glass was drowned by the booming .45-caliber pistol. Shots reverberated like cannon blasts in the enclosed space.

The man in the mirror suddenly disappeared as if someone had switched off his image.

Silently, Bolan stepped from behind Pinolla, right through the empty frame of a destroyed mirror.

The warrior clamped a powerful arm around Pinolla's thick neck, choking off the guy's breath. The mobster heaved backward, the maneuver catching the Executioner unprepared, and the two men tumbled to the glass-strewn floor. The Fatman landed on top, driving the wind from Bolan's lungs.

The mobster scrambled to his feet, trying to bring Bolan into target acquisition.

Bolan lunged with his foot, hard, and caught Pinolla full in his huge stomach, but the mobster merely grunted and swung his gun hand slowly toward Bolan. He smiled evilly, realizing that he had the upper hand.

Bolan groped for something, anything, to use as a weapon. His hand closed on the edge of a long shard of mirror. In a flash he jammed the sharp fragment of glass under Pinolla's chin and ripped.

The Fatman screamed in pain and fell to the floor, spurting blood from his savaged throat. The pistol turned toward the warrior and one last shot blasted from the gun, fanning Bolan's cheek.

Pinolla flopped back. A final spasm rattled the mound of flesh and the Fatman lay still.

Bolan stood and sighed tiredly. The killing ground was in sharp contrast to the gay carousel music blaring from speakers above his head.

Fun, the Executioner mused wryly as he looked around. He wondered briefly about the screams of delight and mock fear that would soon reverberate in the fun house, if the stench of death would somehow linger there.

Bolan gave it up. It was time to leave this place.

More than action adventure...
books written by the men who were there

VIETNAM: GROUND ZERO™

ERIC HELM

Told through the eyes of an American Special Forces squad, an elite jungle fighting group of strike-and-hide specialists fight a dirty war half a world away from home.

These books cut close to the bone, telling it the way it really was.

"Vietnam at Ground Zero is where this book is written. The author has been there, and he knows. I salute him and I recommend this book to my friends."

—Don Pendleton
creator of *The Executioner*

"Helm writes in an evocative style that gives us Nam as it most likely was, without prettying up or undue bitterness."

—*Cedar Rapids Gazette*

"Eric Helm's Vietnam series embodies a literary standard of excellence. These books linger in the mind long after their reading."

—*Midwest Book Review*

Available wherever paperbacks are sold.

VIE-1

by GAR WILSON

The battle-hardened five-man commando unit known as Phoenix Force continues its onslaught against the hard realities of global terrorism in an endless crusade for freedom, justice and the rights of the individual. Schooled in guerrilla warfare, equipped with the latest in lethal weapons, Phoenix Force's adventures have made them a legend in their own time. Phoenix Force is the free world's foreign legion!

"Gar Wilson is excellent! Raw action attacks the reader on every page."
—Don Pendleton

Phoenix Force titles are available wherever paperbacks are sold.

PF-1R

PHOENIX FORCE

GOLD EAGLE

Introducing Max Horn. He's not your typical cop. But then, nothing's typical in the year 2025.

HORN

HOT ZONE

BEN SLOANE

The brutal attack left New York Police Detective Max Horn clinging to life and vowing to seek vengeance on the manic specter who murdered his wife and young son. Now, thanks to cold hard cash and the genius of an underground techno-doc, Max is a new man with a few new advantages—titanium skin and biomechanical limbs hard-wired to his central nervous system.

On an asteroid called New Pittsburgh, Max walks a new beat...and in a horrible twist of fate comes face-to-face with the man who killed his family.